Riley & Scoops

An Evening with Principal Wentworth

Joseph Mirelle

TO MY CHILDREN

1

IT BEGINS

"This is the most boring school in the world," Riley Kushinski whispered under his breath. "Even the dismissal bell lulls students to sleep."

He raised his voice, so it carried across the small office.

"You see Principal Wentworth…" he paused to reflect on how suitable it was that his dull school had such a blah principal. "I don't believe you understand. I just figured Mr. Dil"— he paused, catching himself just in time— "I just thought Mr. Tillweed would find it humorous and it would lighten up his lecture on cytoplasmic organelles."

He sighed and continued with the closing argument in the case he was pleading as if he bore the weight of all his fellow students' misery on his shoulders. "I mean, I think I speak for everyone sir, cellular metabolic functions isn't really riveting stuff you know?"

"We trust our students here, Mr. Kushinski," Principal Wentworth replied sternly. "That is why we have elected to make free-standing water coolers available in every room."

He raised his finger to point out the location of the dispenser in his office but quickly stopped when he remembered there wasn't one. "We treat our students like they deserve to be treated, like adults." He pushed up his thick glasses. "Do you want to ruin these privileges for all your John Smith High School classmates?"

"You're an adult," Riley said defiantly, "do you care about mitochondria and where things you can't see get their energy from?"

Challenged, Principal Wentworth shifted uncomfortably, scratching under his collar while he leaned back slowly in his leather chair. His white, coffee stained, button-up stretched tight across his bulging stomach. Each button strained to keep his shirt fastened while his tie lay effortlessly, barely cresting the summit of his mountain of a belly. The oversized man pawed at his gut like a grizzly bear.

Riley squinted, anticipating the shirt's thin threads and stitching had met their threshold. He gripped the arms of his chair as he anxiously waited for the shirt to explode and shower the room with button shrapnel.

Principal Wentworth exhaled slowly, careful not to overreact or raise his voice. "In fact, I do find that interesting."

Riley ran his fingers through his tight dark curls and mumbled under his breath, "what a surprise."

Principal Wentworth heard him but continued as if he hadn't. "What I also find intriguing is how you found it so amusing to swap the colours of the push taps on your classroom's water cooler so Mr. Tillweed would dispense hot water rather than cold." The big man slowly took a wrinkled handkerchief out of the pocket of his suit coat and blew his nose. He then carefully folded it and slipped it into his chest pocket.

Gross Riley thought, what is with old people and handkerchiefs?

"Scalding hot water," a tall, shell of a man snapped as he stepped forward from the corner of the muggy office. The man donned an old brown suit, blue loafers, and a miserable disposition. He held a wet rag full of ice cubes to his lips as he spoke, "I drank boiling water." He shot a hateful look in Riley's direction then slowly stuck his tongue out to lick the cool fabric in his hand.

"You are supposed to sip hot water, Mr. Tillweed," Riley gently advised. "Not guzzle."

"Really!" Mr. Tillweed shot back steaming, "is—"

"Mr. Tillweed!" Principal Wentworth interrupted immediately leaping in to defuse the situation. "I think what Mr. Kushinski intends to say is that he is very sorry." He looked at Riley for confirmation. "Isn't that correct Mr. Kushinski?"

"Yes, of course," Riley replied apathetically, "I am truly sorry, sir." He paused and looked around the small office, briefly stopping to focus on a small picture of what appeared to be the Principal conducting a large orchestra.

Mr. Tillweed leaned forward in anticipation.

Riley continued, "That you took a massive gulp of hot water."

The tall man had reached his boiling point, "well I'd have half a mind to—" He stopped just before he crossed a line he couldn't step back over again.

"Half of mind, sir?" Riley snickered, "I hear we only use half our brain, so there is not much going on up there is there?" He pointed to his head while looking at the Principal as if he would appreciate his humour.

Mr. Tillweed stepped forward and hissed, "why you—"

"That will be all Mr. Tillweed." Principal Wentworth interrupted again. "I will continue to chat with Mr. Kushinski."

Recognizing he was not going to receive the satisfaction of a verbal apology, Mr. Tillweed flailed his arms up in the air and stomped out of the room fuming. The wet cloth in his hand spraying water all over the Principal's office.

"Mr. Kushinski," Principal Wentworth warned as he leaned forward, pressing his fingertip gently on some of the newly formed water droplets that had landed on his mahogany desk. "You must understand that here at this school we do not tolerate this sort of…" he paused unbelieving what he was about to say, "Deviant behaviour. Even more importantly…" he paused for dramatic effect then flicked at a giant water bubble as if was a spec of dirt, "your refusal to obey the authority of your teachers is something that at I assure you, will be addressed immediately."

His attempt to intimidate Riley failed as the droplet moved less than an inch and split in two.

"Powerful stuff, sir."

The Principal's eyes lit up as he thought that he might have expressed his point.

"Cohesion and adhesion," Riley clarified. "Powerful stuff."

Principal Wentworth sighed, accepting his efforts were fruitless and continued to discipline. Riley just nodded like a bobblehead and pretended to listen when in fact he was preoccupied trying to read the

Principal's crooked diplomas barely hanging in the corner above a dented and rusting filing cabinet.

Principal Wentworth blabbered on as if he had Riley's full attention until there was a knock on the door. He stopped his muttering and put his hands on the desk to push his chair back. He grunted as he stood up. "What now?"

As he waddled to the door, Riley studied him. He must have been only in his mid-fifties but looked like he was pushing seventy. The top of his head was bald and the hair still surviving was unkempt. His suit was far too small and his shirt desperately in need of a good press, not to mention a few more inches. He had a slight limp which Riley thought could be attributed to the fact that his shoes didn't look like they matched.

"Yes?" he asked as he flung open the door.

Standing feebly on the other side was the school secretary Ms. Fitzpatrick. She wore a frayed burgundy cardigan over a fatigued flower patterned dress. She was far too elderly to have a job, however, could handle the workload because not unlike Mr. Tillweed's sense of humour, it did not exist. Nothing ever happened at John Smith High School.

"Excuse me, Principal Wentworth," she spoke timidly in a thick British accent. She peered over her horn-rimmed bifocals. "I am sorry to interrupt."

"That is fine, Ms. Fitzpatrick, what is it?" he replied softly. The old woman just stared back at him as if she had forgotten why she knocked. He waited a couple of seconds then prodded. "Ms. Fitzpatrick?"

"Oh, yes. Sorry sir," she looked as though he had just woken her up. "I am sorry to interrupt."

"That is ok, Ms. Fitzpatrick, what is it?" Principal Wentworth insisted.

She continued as she fingered an old butterfly brooch, "oh, well, I am sorry to interrupt, but we have…"

Just as it seemed she was about to get it out, Riley saw the opportunity to disrupt her momentum. He stood up and walked briskly over to the door as if to say hi to an old friend. "Greetings Ms. Fitz, how are you?" he sang.

Startled, she reset.

"Oh hi," she stuttered, "sorry to interrupt."

"No problem Ms. Fitz," Riley said cheerfully mimicking her accent. "Principal Wentworth and I are just having a good chin wag."

"Riley sit down!" Principal Wentworth barked. "What is it, Ms. Fitzpatrick?" he asked. His pitch revealed he was becoming increasingly annoyed with the situation.

Riley ignored Principal Wentworth and stepped forward with an outstretched arm to shake Ms. Fitzpatrick's hand. "It's good to see you, Ms. Fitz. How's your cat Mr. Wiggles, still holding down the Fitzpatrick fort?"

"Mr. Wiggles?" she asked perplexed. "Well, I don't remember." She stared up at the moldy ceiling tiles deep in thought as Riley gently shook her hand.

Content with both the confusion on Ms. Fitzpatrick's face as well as the frustration in Principal Wentworth's voice Riley jovially returned to his seat as instructed. "Well say hi to him when you find him," he said as he sat down. "Cute little helpless thing, isn't he?"

"Yes, yes," she replied. "I will be sure to pass on your regards when I find him, that poor helpless dear." She turned to leave completely, forgetting the reason she knocked.

"Ms. Fitzpatrick!" Principal Wentworth yelled. "You knocked?"

"Oh yes, yes, indeed. I am sorry to interrupt. But..."

"Yes?" Principal Wentworth jumped in to hurry her along.

"Well, we have a new student here today," she muttered. "His name is Mr. Wiggles. Would you like me to show him in?"

"Mr. Wiggles?" Principal Wentworth replied baffled, his eyebrows raised, and his glasses slid down the bridge of his nose.

"Yes, I think so," she replied, "Mr. Wiggles, I do believe. Well, actually, I can't remember."

Out of nowhere, a young boy bounded past her into the room. His shaggy blonde hair wisped in the breeze of his swift pace. He was light on his feet and full of energy. "Not Mr. Wiggles, sir," he proclaimed, "I believe that is the missing feline."

He paused as though he was grieving, "poor helpless thing."

He continued with an outstretched hand, "name's Jack Floyd sir. It's a pleasure to meet you."

Principal Wentworth reciprocated, and the slim boy greeted him with a firm handshake that almost ripped his already heavily taxed suit coat at the seams.

The newcomer continued into the office and helped himself to an open chair next to Riley. He gave Riley a hearty slap on the shoulder that almost popped the collar up on his light blue polo.

"Hi there, great to meet you," he said as he brushed his hair out of his blue eyes. He offered Riley his outstretched hand, "name is Jack Floyd, but my friends call me Scoops."

"Scoops?" Riley asked bewildered. As he appraised Scoops' outfit, he thought to himself, who is this guy?

Scoops wore a pair of faded, ripped blue jeans and a timeworn blue and white striped sweater. His sense of style was awful, and he was a sight for sore eyes.

Principal Wentworth slowly paced in the corner of the office. His hands clenched into tight fists. He tried to calm down, but it was no use.

Ms. Fitzpatrick had left the office. In the other room, you could hear her calling, "Wiggles, oh Mr. Wiggles."

Irritated, Principal Wentworth removed his suit coat revealing two gigantic sweat stains under his armpits. He threw the coat on top of the filing cabinet, stirring up a cloud of dust and made his way back to the office door. As he swung it open, he shouted at the top of his lungs. "Ms. Fitzpatrick, please bring me a coffee with cream and sugar!"

He turned and faced the boys.

"Riley I want you to write a formal letter of apology to Mr. Tillweed."

"Mr. Tillweed," Scoops giggled and looked at Riley. "Kind of sounds like dill weed."

Riley laughed, "I know, right. That is what I've been saying." They chuckled in unison while Principal Wentworth dropped his head in his hands.

"Why a letter?" Scoops grilled Mr. Wentworth. "Maybe he can just give him a call?"

Scoops was comfortably immersing himself in the conversation as if it was just as much his business as Riley's.

Riley nodded in agreement, "Yeah, good idea, I wonder what his number is?"

"I will look him up." Scoops pulled his phone from the pocket of his jeans eager to help, "how do you spell dill weed?"

Principal Wentworth watched as the boys carried on as if they were the only ones in the room. After a few seconds, he attempted to re-establish his authority. "We don't allow phones in class, Mr. Floyd."

Scoops looked around studying the wood panels on the walls of the dimly lit office and quickly dismissed him. "Sorry, sir, but I am not in class."

"Try dialing zero, that is probably his direct line," Riley suggested.

They both chuckled.

"Gentlemen!" Principal Wentworth shouted. When he had attracted their full attention, he continued. "Mr. Floyd, would you kindly butt out."

The boys snickered.

"Sorry Principal Wentworth, kindly what out?" Scoops asked with a smile strewn across his face.

"Butt!" Principal Wentworth erupted.

The boys laughed hysterically.

Principal Wentworth slammed his fists on his desk, the blow sending his pen bouncing off the desk to the floor just as Ms. Fitzpatrick pushed open the door carrying a small tray with a coffee and single creamer on it. She sensed the tension in the room and stopped quickly.

"Sorry Principal Wentworth, here is your coffee," she softly whispered as she looked at the two boys who were still giggling. She shuffled slowly over to the desk and set the tray down. Her hand shaking as it placed a coffee mug covered in music notes and some writing on an old coaster. She then took a small Coffee-mate creamer out of her sweater pocket and put it upside down on the desk.

Riley leaned forward and read the cup. "Conductors Know How to Give Musicians Good Time."

"I like to have," Scoops replaced the 'a' with a pause, "good time."

As she was about to leave Ms. Fitzpatrick turned to Principal Wentworth. "You look upset, is everything alright?"

Principal Wentworth growled and waved her off.

"Some people can be so easily irritated," Scoops said. Then with the confidence of an experienced sleep specialist consulted, "a person needs to get a solid eight hours a night."

"Too much caffeine probably," Riley suggested. "I hope this coffee is decaf."

"Ms. Fitzpatrick," Principal Wentworth called out to catch her before she left, "I am missing sugar. Could you please grab me some?"

"Oh yes, I'm so sorry," she apologized. "I will go find some right away."

"Look next to Mr. Wiggles," Scoops suggested.

"Mr. Wiggles, that's an excellent idea," Ms. Fitzpatrick replied and slowly left the room, closing the door softly behind her.

"Where were we?" Principal Wentworth asked as the door clicked shut, and he returned his bloodshot gaze on the two boys.

Riley watched in horror as he reached into his chest pocket and pulled his soiled handkerchief back out, unfolded it and wiped the beading sweat off his forehead. Riley's face continued to contort in disgust as he folded the cloth again and returned it to his shirt pocket. He was too disturbed to comment.

"Butt I think sir, you were on butt," Scoops reminded him.

Principal Wentworth shook his head adamantly. "No, I was not."

He waited for the boys to stop laughing before continuing.

"Kushinski, you will write a letter of apology to Mr. Tillweed, by good old-fashioned pen and paper." As he spoke, he began fingering around his desk.

"Looking for a spoon, sir?" Riley asked.

"Nevermind!" Principal Wentworth shot back.

Scoops reached onto the desk and grabbed a fiberglass stick. "How about this, sir?" he asked, doing his best to come off as concerned and helpful as possible.

Principal Wentworth snatched the stick out of Scoops' hand as if he had just tried to steal his wallet.

"What's that?" Riley asked.

"A chopstick?" Scoops replied. He looked around on the floor. Where is the other one, sir?"

"It's a baton!" Principal Wentworth growled.

"You twirl, sir?" Riley asked, surprised.

"No, I do not twirl," he roared defensively, "it is for conducting a band."

"I don't know anything about music, sir," Scoops informed him.

The Principal rolled his eyes and ignored him. "Where is she?" he asked, growing more impatient with every degree his coffee cooled.

Again, he placed both hands on his desk, rolling his chair away. He habitually groaned as he pushed himself up. He thundered over to the door, flung it open and left the room, calling for his elderly secretary.

When he was out of sight, Scoops reached forward and grabbed the small creamer that sat innocently on the desk before them. Riley watched as Scoops continued to hold the small container upside down and use a small paperclip to poke a tiny hole through the plastic just above the cream. Scoops then carefully placed it back on the desk with the small hole towards them. The hole was barely visible above the cream you could see through the translucent plastic.

"Kushinski," Scoops said to Riley calmly. "Sounds Russian or something."

"Riley shrugged, "I don't know."

Scoops scrunched his lips. "Sorry you lost the race to the moon, you guys were so close."

"I'm not Russian," Riley protested, "my name might be, but I don't even know that for sure." Riley scratched his head and then pulled on a swirl of dark curls. "All I do know is that I was born here, my parents were too."

Scoops studied Riley's sharp features, brown hair, and eyes. "Never be ashamed of who you are Riley." He sounded genuinely concerned. "You should be proud. You Russians have warm hats, cool tanks, and those cute little doll things with a bunch of other tiny dolls inside them."

"Aren't those from the Netherlands?" Riley asked.

"Nope, that was the Lost Boys," Scoops answered confidently. "The Lost Boys are from the Netherlands. And Peter Pan." He sat nodding as if he was defending a thesis. "Not sure about Wendy, though. Not sure where she lived. Maybe she is from Russia?"

"I am not from Russia, Scoops!" Riley shifted in his seat and shook his head, "and I said the Netherlands, not Never Land."

"Same thing I think," Scoops replied. "Anyway, I'm pretty sure those nesting doll thingies are Russian too. Your mom probably has some put away in a box in the attic. Convenient little things, they pretty much pack themselves."

Principal Wentworth charged back into the room with a spoon and a small packet of sugar. He sat down hard in his chair and attempted to wheel himself forward with his feet. Besides a lot of squeaking and heavy breathing, no movement occurred. He sighed heavily flopping the spoon and sugar on the desk. He grunted as he used his desk to pull himself forward until his belly nudged up against it.

When finally settled, he ripped the small packet and poured the sugar into his coffee then snatched up the creamer. As he flipped the creamer over to peel the lid off, cream began to flow out of the small hole Scoops made. "What am I going to do with you two?" he asked with both his eyes fixated on the two boys.

Meanwhile, a steady stream of French Vanilla liquid creamer poured all over his tie and stomach. The stream was too weak for him to feel, and it went undetected. When he had finished peeling back the lid, he threw it in a small wastebasket on the floor.

He picked up the stirring spoon as he turned to pour the cream into his coffee. The creamer was empty. "What the...?" His words dissipated as he saw the cream all over his shirt and tie, as did his patience and restraint. He slammed the empty creamer against his desk, and it skipped across the room. "Why you..." he snarled at the two boys grinning like idiots across from him.

"Looks like you got a bad one, sir," Riley said. "It must have been a factory defect." He looked at Scoops, "I wonder who they have running quality control over there at Nestle these days?"

"Or haven't," Scoops pointed out.

They both chuckled.

Principal Wentworth snapped. "Both of you, detention now!"

"Detention," Riley's mouth dropped. "I don't think we have a detention room, sir."

Principal Wentworth stopped to think, the kid was right, he had never sent anyone to detention before. He fumbled through his desk drawers, looking for something to wipe himself off.

"Ms. Fitzpatrick!" he screamed.

The boys jumped.

They stared at Wentworth as he pointed at them and scolded. "You two will be the first to have detention at John Smith High School."

"Really?" Scoops asked, smiling as if awarded a badge of honour he would wear proudly.

"What about the quality control guy at the creamery?" Riley asked, still pleading their innocence. "What does he get?"

Ms. Fitzpatrick had finally made her way to the door. "Yes, Principal Wentworth?" she asked. Her eyes drifted to the Principal's wet shirt. "Oh sir, did you spill your coffee?"

"Creamer," Scoops supplied.

"Factory defect," Riley added. "Probably packaged on a Monday or Friday."

"Can you please get me a cloth?" Principal Wentworth asked. "Or anything you can find to wipe this up with," frustration dominated his voice. "And please find a place for these two boys to serve detention."

"Detention, sir?" she asked puzzled. "I don't think we have ever had one of those before."

"We have now!" he barked back at her. "Find these two a place they can sit the rest of the day where they will read and complete a book report on a book I choose." He stopped, "No wait," he pointed to Ms. Fitzpatrick, "a book that you pick. That ought to be good." He chuckled to himself, reveling in his idea.

"Oh, that sounds fun," Ms. Fitzpatrick responded, "how very delightful."

Principal Wentworth shook his head in disapproval, "No, Ms. Fitzpatrick, this is intended to be punishment."

"Punishment," she gasped. "Oh dear, why do you intend to punish these lovely young boys?"

"And on my first day," Scoops whined.

"Yeah quite the orientation," Riley joined in and then went into a tirade, "how was your first day son? Met the Principal, he was pleasant but having a bit of an off day. Then they stuck me in a room to read a book all day. I didn't get to see much of the school. Only met one kid.

15

He was super cool. How was your day, dad? Pretty good. I started my new job at the creamery, but the quality control guy was as useless as a comb in a Tibetan Monastery, so I had to fire him. Luckily I solved that issue before it caused any serious problems."

Ms. Fitzpatrick listened attentively, "oh how wonderful, your father sounds like a great man." She was completely oblivious to the fact that Riley had ad-libbed his entire rant.

"Out! Out! Everybody out!" Principal Wentworth screeched. "I can't take this anymore. Ms. Fitzpatrick, take these boys to the library and tell Miss Carpenter to stuff them into a study room where I don't have to see them for the rest of the day!"

He stopped, gasping for breath. "Get them out of my office now!"

"Sounds good Principal Wentworth," Scoops said enthusiastically. "What book are we reading?"

"That is up to Ms. Fitzpatrick."

"Oh boys, I have a good one," Ms. Fitzpatrick said, interlocking her arthritic fingers in excitement. She began to summarize. "It is called The Blue Lagoon. It is a lovely story about two people that get stranded on a deserted island."

"Kind of like two boys being stranded in a small room all day," Riley lamented.

"Oh boys, I am sorry," she said sympathetically. "I never thought of that, my apologies you poor things."

"How about something a little lighter, like a magazine or something?" Riley suggested.

Scoops piped up. "Or a comic."

Principal Wentworth put his foot down. "You two will read Blue Lagoon, no ifs ands or buts."

He reached down, picked up the baton off his desk, and pointed it at them. "Now get to the library."

"But what if The Blue Lagoon is signed out?" Scoops asked, doing his best to sound as worried as possible. "Sounds like a real page-turner, sir?"

"Ifs, ands, or whats?" Riley asked giggling.

"Out! Out! Out!" Principal Wentworth bellowed as he stood frantically waving the baton like a sorcerer's wand herding Ms. Fitzpatrick and the boys out of his office.

2
DETENTION

The boys sat imprisoned in a small room in the back of John Smith High School's tiny library. Although small, the library was bright and cheerful, filled with natural light from large windows that lined the wall overlooking the sports fields and track. The boys slumped in their plastic chairs staring at a copy of The Blue Lagoon and a stack of loose-leaf paper.

"Henry De Vere Stacpoole," Riley read aloud. "My eyes are already tired reading the author's name."

Scoops clicked his pen repeatedly and stared across the table at his new best friend. He took a short hiatus, then tried to twirl the pen through his fingers but ended up flinging it across the room. It bounced off a motivational picture that looked more suited for a funeral program cover than inspiring the future leaders of tomorrow. Scoops stood and read the quote on the poster. He nodded as if he was taking a mental note. He then bent down awkwardly to pick up his pen. Riley watched as he squeezed himself between the table and a chair.

Scoops stepped back away from the poster as if it were a 3D stereogram and if he stood in just the right place, refusing to blink it would all make sense to him. "Have you read this book before?" he asked.

"Nope," Riley responded matter-of-factly.

"Too bad," Scoops said disappointedly. "You could have saved us some time there."

Riley rationalized with him, "well, it doesn't look like we are getting out of here anytime soon anyway."

They both looked out the glass wall that separated them from the rest of the vacant library. There was not a single soul in the place except Miss Carpenter who sat behind the front counter scanning in books from the return cart. She was in her early thirties, fit and her long straight blonde hair hung all the way down to her hips in a ponytail. She wore a navy-blue V-neck cardigan over a white blouse tucked neatly into a pair of tight-fitting white denim jeans. The outfit was suited more for an evening on the town than an empty library with two teenage boys and thousands of similarly overlooked novels. Riley and Scoops watched her thinking the same thing but hesitant to admit it.

Scoops was the first to break out of his trance. "Quite the place," he murmured. He surveyed the rows of dusty books in the empty library, "so many words but so little sound."

Riley let out a suppressive sigh, "wow that is pretty deep, Scoops."

"Yeah," Scoops said, sounding quite surprised himself. He blew the hair out of his eyes, "I just don't know where it comes from sometimes."

"Speaking of somewhere," Riley said suddenly, "where are you from?" He took his eyes off the librarian and looked across the table at Scoops. "What's your deal?"

"My deal?" Scoops asked, pointing to himself as if there was someone else in the room.

"Yeah," Riley said nodding, "what brought you to Bridgeport?"

Scoops shuffled in his seat and appeared disinterested. "My dad got a new job."

"Really, where at?" Riley asked.

"Just at Nestle," he paused to let it sink in, "he's responsible for quality control."

"Really?" Riley asked wide-eyed.

Scoops laughed. "No, my dad's a lawyer."

"Really?"

"Yeah, really," Scoops nodded.

Riley was delighted. "Huh, my dad is too."

"Really?" Scoops asked, surprised. He had transitioned from the interviewee to the interviewer.

"Yep works at RH Johnson and Associates or something like that," Riley, announced proudly.

"Really?"

"Yep."

"Interesting," Scoops noted. "I think my dad works at a Johnson place too."

"Really?" Riley asked as their roles in the interview swapped again. "What's your mom do?"

"She just stays home."

"She's a homemaker," Riley said nodding.

Scoops shook his head from side to side. "Nope, she couldn't build a gingerbread house, she hates construction. Me too, I wouldn't last a day outside in the winter."

"No, I mean, homemaker. That's what you call it I think," Riley explained. "You know, looks after the kids, makes lunches, does chores, and runs errands—"

"Watches soaps for a living," Scoops interrupted. "Yeah, that's her." Then he added casually under his breath. "Sometimes she works at a diner too."

He looked back out the window at Miss Carpenter then back at Riley. "What does your mom do?"

"She is a homemaker too," Riley answered. He had heard but decided to ignore the diner comment getting the sense Scoops didn't want to talk about it.

"Really?" Scoops asked.

"Really."

"I didn't realize that many women liked to build houses."

Riley stared at Scoops blank-faced.

After a few seconds, Scoops cracked a smile, "I'm just kidding."

They laughed together and resumed goggling Miss Carpenter as she laboriously scanned books back into the system.

"Nice place for detention," Riley noted. "It's kind of like getting the ocean view balcony at Chateau d'if."

"Chateau d'if?" Scoops asked, confused.

"Ever seen Count of Monte Cristo?"

21

"Yeah, that was a great show." He picked his copy of The Blue Lagoon off the table and fanned the pages. Wish someone would have written a book based on that movie." Scoops sighed and tossed the book back on the table as if it was a horseshoe.

They still hadn't read a word.

Riley left Scoops book comment alone. "Old Edmond Dantes wasn't the forgiving type, hey?"

Scoops tilted his head, pondering Riley's question but never responded. Instead, he returned it with one of his own. "Do you think you can ever forgive Principal Wentworth for sticking us in here?"

Riley laughed, "I'm not sure that is comparable."

"Yeah, I guess he's just having an off day," Scoops said as if the Principal's decision to exile them required justification. "What do you want to do today?"

"What do you mean?" Riley asked.

"Well, you don't think we are just going to stay here all day, do you?"

"Well, we are in detention."

"It's my first day," Scoops reminded Riley. "I want to break out of here like the Count."

"Well, what are we going to do about Miss Carpenter?" Riley pointed at the attractive robot across the library. She looked as though she had completely dozed off, but somehow her hands still moved repetitively.

"She won't even notice. Look at her," Scoops told Riley as he pointed, "she will probably be busy scanning all afternoon, and we'll be the ones checked out of here."

He smiled at his pun.

"As soon as she goes to put those books back on the shelves we'll make a break for it." Scoops spoke as if he had been part of a dozen successful prison breaks.

"What if Principal Wentworth comes to check on us?"

"I am sure he is not interested in seeing us anymore," Scoops replied with confidence. "If he does, we will just have to say we had to use the bathroom." He looked around the room. "It is not our fault this cell is lacking the facilities that we require to perform such basic but necessary human bodily functions." He continued to rant, "nope, not our fault, much like his wardrobe. I don't think he has put much thought into this detention thing at all."

"And what about our book report?" Riley asked.

"That old thing," Scoops answered as he walked to the glass wall to get a closer look at Miss Carpenter. "When we get out of here we can just look up what The Blue Lagoon is all about." He scratched his head. Then ran his fingers through his long blonde locks. "How do they expect us to read that whole book anyway?"

Miss Carpenter broke out of her hypnotic state and looked around the library as if she had heard a sound.

"Do you think she even remembers we are in here?" Riley asked Scoops.

"I don't know," Scoops replied. "What else does she have to think about?"

Miss Carpenter raised her hand slowly to her face as she looked around. She started scratching the bridge of her nose with her right thumb and forefinger while her left hand massaged the back of her neck.

"She must," Riley said as they watched her all dreamy-eyed. "We have only been in here for an hour."

"Probably seems like a lifetime to her," Scoops said. He looked at Riley and asked, "Who is taking all these books out anyway?"

Miss Carpenter took another careful look around the library as if she was searching for peeping toms. Before the boys could anticipate it, she stopped rubbing her nose and stuck her finger in her nostril.

"Eww," Riley gasped, "no way."

"I don't think she remembers we are in here," Scoops confirmed.

The boy held their breath as Miss Carpenter pulled her finger from her nose and carefully analyzed it. She then started rubbing the tip of her finger on the inside of her thumb.

"No way," Scoops whispered. "I can't believe it. She's rolling it up."

The boys watched without blinking as the beautiful women stopped and canvassed the library again. She then glanced down at her finger. From across the room, they could make out a gooey tightrope stretching from her finger to her thumb.

"Not having much luck," Riley corrected Scoops, "that doesn't look like the rolling type."

"Nope."

"Sick," Riley said, disgusted.

"She should roll it down her pant leg," Scoops suggested. "That will get the moisture out."

Riley shot him a concerned glance. "Is that what you do?"

"Nope," Scoop replied in a faint whisper. "Of course, not," he lied.

"Phew," Riley exhaled.

"I stick it in my sock."

24

Riley's jaw dropped, "you do what?"

Scoops ignored him as if it was nothing. "I bet she is going to stick it in a book."

"No way," Riley argued, "she wouldn't."

"Ten bucks she does," Scoops proposed.

"No way."

"Yeah way," Scoops persisted.

Miss Carpenter made a fist with the guilty hand, coughed into it and stood up.

"Good move," Scoops said admiringly, "going with the old clench and cleanse."

"What's that?" Riley asked curiously. He didn't know who was worse, Miss Carpenter or Scoops who seemed too well versed on the subject.

"It's Plan B if the pick and flick fails," he calmly said as if it were an instinct Riley didn't have in his DNA.

They watched as Miss Carpenter sashayed out of the library. She flipped her ponytail with her left hand and kept her right arm down by her side. Her right hand looked like it gripped a roll of quarters.

"She is going to the bathroom," Riley said relieved.

"Yep, let's make a break for it."

"Where?" Riley asked.

"I don't know, anywhere but here."

Riley hesitated. "Oh man, I am not sure Scoops," his voice starting to tremor.

"Don't worry," Scoops assured him, "let's go." He gave Riley the nod. "I am not spending my first day at Bore High stuck in this tiny room."

Riley sighed and shook his head in defeat. "Ok, let's go." He went to grab the doorknob then quickly stopped. He paused second-guessing his decision.

Scoops brushed past Riley before he could change his mind. He grabbed the knob and slowly pushed open the door. Then he stuck his head out and looked around the quiet library. When he was satisfied there was no one watching, he turned back to Riley who was standing right behind him peering over his shoulder. "Let's go!"

3
THE GREAT ESCAPE

Miss Carpenter was out of the library, but the boys tiptoed as if she was still in earshot. They ducked and covered through the rows of non-fiction books and rolled their way over to the fiction section as if they were breaking out of a high-security prison. When they reached the entrance to the library, Scoops dropped down to peek through the crack between the wood door and old worn out carpet. He peered down the hallway. His cheek squashed against the dirty floor. "Looks clear," he mumbled. "Which way are we going?"

"I don't know," Riley replied from behind him shrugging. "This is your idea."

"Yeah, I know," Scoops whispered at the top of his lungs. "But I don't know where to go?"

Riley quickly covered Scoops mouth and shushed him.

Scoops ripped Riley's hand off his face and struggled back to his feet. "This is my first day, remember?"

Riley rolled his eyes. "Ok, I will lead."

Just as Riley was about to open the door, it started to swing open towards them. The boys gasped and instinctively pushed it closed with their backs then planted the soles of their shoes deep into the carpet to hold it shut.

"Oh, man!" Riley panicked. "What do we do?"

"Hey, what's going on in there?" a male voice boomed from the other side.

Riley immediately recognized it. "It's Mr. Tillweed."

Scoops laughed. "Ha-ha Tillweed."

Riley's fear-ridden face cracked into a smile.

"What is going on in there?" Mr. Tillweed yelled. "Is everything alright?" He pushed on the door again.

The boys held steady.

"Open this door immediately!" Mr. Tillweed thundered.

Scoops looked at Riley and motioned to step aside.

Mr. Tillweed lunged at the door. Without the boys' weight against it, the door flung open. He flew into the library, crashing into a nearby display then came to rest in a pile of hardcovers.

"That is one way to dive into a book," Scoops quipped.

"What in tarnation!" Tillweed yelled as he tried to scramble to his feet. The originality continued. "What in blue blazes is going on in here?"

Riley acted fast.

"Sorry, Mr. Tillweed," he said casually as if he just beat him to the salad prongs in a buffet line. "I was just giving our newest student a tour of the school. I couldn't think of a better place to start than the library."

"And why was the door locked?" he snarled, attempting to replace his look of confusion with control.

"It wasn't," Scoops inserted as if Riley had tagged him into the ring. "We were holding it shut."

His candid answer shocked everyone in the room. Riley sent Scoops a dirty look as Tillweed erupted.

"Why would you be holding it shut?" He looked around as if he was looking for hostages. "Where's Miss Carpenter?"

"She left," Riley replied coolly.

Mr. Tillweed looked around the library as if Riley was lying and he was about to find her tied up in an aisle. His search and rescue efforts yielded no clues to her whereabouts. "Well, where did she go?" he asked anxiously.

"I think she had a delivery," Scoops replied.

"What kind of delivery?"

"A small one, sir," Scoops smirked.

"Yep, very small, sir," Riley contributed, looking out across the library to make sure he did not crack a smile.

"And why were you two holding the door shut?" he asked again sharply.

"Well, that is another story," Riley said as if the full narrative would bore the teacher.

"What's the story, Riley?" Mr. Tillweed howled.

Scoops was busy picking carpet fuzz off his sweater from his army crawl across the library floor. "It is complicated sir," he interjected.

Mr. Tillweed's brow wrinkled. "Complicated?" he asked, slack-jawed as if someone told him to recite the periodic table starting with alloys. He turned to Riley flabbergasted looking for some explanation. "What, is he talking about, and who is he again?"

Mr. Tillweed was clearly not seeing the full picture, in fact, missing the entire gallery.

"I am John Smith's newest student," Scoops boasted. He extended his hand to shake Tillweed's. "The name is Scoops, sir."

The gesture startled Tillweed. "Oh hi," the drab man replied awkwardly extending his hand. "I'm Mr. Tillweed."

"Great to meet you, Mr. Dill Weed," Scoops responded quickly.

"Tillweed," he corrected Scoops as they shook hands.

"My mistake," Scoops said sympathetically, "sorry sir." He sighed. "That would be rather unfortunate, wouldn't it?"

He continued as he looked passed the tall teacher down the empty corridor as if he had somewhere else to go. "Won't happen again," Scoops assured him. "Well, we best continue with the tour Riley."

The boys tried to push past the tall teacher.

"Wait a minute," Tillweed said, blocking their exit. "Why were you holding the door shut?"

"That is another story, sir," Scoops repeated as if they had told it a thousand times.

"What's the story?" Mr. Tillweed demanded.

"Well," Riley stuttered, struggling to find something clever to say.

Scoops threw him a lifeline. "Riley was just going through fire safety procedure, sir."

Tillweed dropped his chin to his chest, closing his eyes and raising his eyebrows slowly. He exhaled, "fire safety?" He began rubbing the back of his neck as if he had a migraine.

Riley clued in. "Yes, I was running through what we are supposed to do if there is a fire. We are to make sure to shut the doors, so oxygen doesn't heat up the fire and causes it to spread faster." Riley started to lecture, "It's kind of like how mitochondria get energy, and the cells multiply and stuff."

Tillweed shook his head in disbelief and looked as though he wanted to extinguish Riley. "What do you know?" he muttered.

Just then, Miss Carpenter walked up behind Mr. Tillweed. As she saw the two boys, she remembered she was supposed to be watching them.

She glanced at Mr. Tillweed, then Riley and Scoops. "What are you boys doing out of detention?" she asked.

"Detention?" Tillweed repeated surprised. He wasn't sure if he should be angry that the boys had been lying, or happy about Riley Kushinski's sentence.

Scoops didn't miss a beat. "Hi, Miss Carpenter," he said cheerfully. "Great to see you again, everything ok?"

She was startled. "Yes, by all means, what are you talking about?"

"That's good," Scoops responded as if it were nothing. "You were just gone a while, so we started to worry about you." He looked at Mr. Tillweed and tried to appear as concerned as possible, "so we wanted to find you and make sure you were alright."

"Yes, I am fine," she said as she looked at her tall colleague.

"Great to hear," Scoops said. "We were worried you got yourself in a sticky situation."

Scoops looked at Riley and smiled.

"Everything is fine," she replied. Trying to figure out what was going on. Then it hit her. They were in the study room and must have been watching her the whole time. Her face went white. Her best defense was a strong offense. "You boys better get back into detention, or I will go get Principal Wentworth."

"Detention," Tillweed echoed softly, staring at the ceiling as if an orchestra of angels had just descended out of the heavens playing the most beautiful music he had ever heard.

"Yes, detention," Scoops repeated, giving his best effort to look convicted and apologetic as if it might lessen their sentence. "We better get back to our book reports." He motioned to the small study, "and you better finish your letter too."

"Letter, what letter?" Tillweed asked quizzically. Curiosity rolled off him like sweat from Principal Wentworth's forehead.

"Your apology letter Mr. Tillweed," Scoops answered as if the science teacher was still writing his hypothesis and the rest of the class had already finished the experiment.

"I see," Tillweed exclaimed, eager to hear more.

"First, we should probably finish the fire drill," Riley chimed in.

"Get back to detention!" Tillweed shouted. He cherished the words as they shot out of his mouth. "I am not a fool."

Miss Carpenter laughed as if to amplify his point.

Riley and Scoops just stared at her blank-faced.

Her laugh irritated Scoops, and he was no longer interested in the exchange. "Ok Riley, let's go," he said bluntly, "back to the mines Miss Carpenter."

He and Riley turned and made their way back to the study room as if they had choreographed a set play.

"Mines?" Tillweed asked Miss Carpenter. "What does that mean?"

Miss Carpenter just ignored him.

4
THE GREAT RELEASE

Back in the stuffy study, the boys' discussion continued. "What's this place like anyway?" Scoops asked.

Riley pondered the question. "Well, let's see. How would I describe this place?" He watched out the window as Mr. Tillweed put his hand on Miss Carpenter's shoulder as if he was comforting her. "Probably a waiting room."

"A waiting room?" Scoops' eyes narrowed.

"Yeah everybody here is just bored, waiting to get out of here. Everyone is scared to talk to each other, and nothing noteworthy ever happens. People just dread being here and look at their watches all day wondering why it feels like more time has passed than has."

"Yikes," Scoops clenched his jaw, "can't think of anything better to describe this place than a waiting room, huh?" His face saddened, "must be a boring place."

Riley could sense his disappointment but had nothing positive to say. "Well, I guess it's not that terrible." He couldn't lie to his new friend. He knew he would find out soon enough. "It's just that the teachers treat the students like they are a burden. They act as if they are a bunch of professors or something completing research that will one day change the world, and the fact that they have to teach is just getting in the way. I don't think they even care about us." He sighed, "And they certainly don't want us to enjoy ourselves."

Riley's behaviour was starting to make a lot more sense to Scoops. He was starting to like this kid. They were kindred spirits, and together, they could do great things.

"Any girls?" Scoops asked hoping to uncover another bright light other than his cellmate.

"Girls?" Riley repeated as if he had never breached the topic with another male student in his life. "Well, yeah," his mood lifted, "a couple."

Scoops face lightened. "Great, you should introduce me."

"Well, I don't actually know them," Riley admitted.

Scoops went into shock. "Don't know them? Why not? What else have you been doing?"

"Well," Riley started to reply. "Well…" he couldn't think of a good response that would appease Scoops and get him off the hook.

"I will tell you," Scoops said to him. "You've been sitting and sulking in the waiting room man, breathing in everybody's fumes pretending to read but really trying to figure out who it is that smells. Meanwhile, if you lifted your head and looked around, you would see it isn't that bad. It's time to put down the crusty germ ridden magazines and turn the waiting room into a dance floor buddy."

"Yeah, you're right," Riley replied, an optimistic smile growing on his face. He changed the subject. "Should we tackle this book report?"

"Absolutely!" Scoops replied. "As soon as you are finished telling me about these," his eyes filled with passion as if he was reciting a romantic sonnet, "girls."

Riley leaned back in his chair, let his head fall back, and stared straight up at the ceiling. He sighed deeply. "Oh man, you are going to be trouble."

Scoops, relentless in his quest to learn more about the girls, ignored the comment, "where are their lockers?"

Riley leaned forward and put his elbows on the table, "book report first, or we're never going to get out of here."

Scoops face dropped, "alright, alright," he stretched his arms high above his head and cracked his knuckles as if he was ready to dive right in.

When the dismissal bell rang, the boys were fast asleep. On the fourth ring, they began to stir. Riley had fallen asleep with his head resting on his folded arms. Scoops lay with his forehead pressed flat against the table, his arms dangling alongside his legs just inches from touching the floor. When he lifted his head off the desk pieces of paper stuck to his brow. He pawed them off like a cat grooming itself.

"We better get this ready for Principal Wentworth," Riley said groggily. He piled up the pages on the desk and peeled the sheets from Scoops' face. "Gross," he said in disgust as the pages stuck together.

Scoops wiped the drool from his cheek with the back of his hand. "A job well done, I would say."

Riley nodded in agreement as he tapped the paper against the desk to line up the edges. When he finished, he laid the stack in a neat pile on the table, then stood and walked to the glass wall. He looked around the library. "Where is Miss Carpenter?"

Scoops stood up and walked over to him. "Not sure, but I really have to go to the bathroom." He squeezed his knees together. "We have been in here all day."

"There she is," Riley said as she came strutting out of a row of books and turned heading in their direction.

"Oops," Scoops said sheepishly.

"What?"

"There has been a small accident."

No further explanation was required. The foulest of odors had saturated the room. "Ahh, how could you?" Riley asked, shoving his nose as far as he could into his elbow. "What did you eat for lunch?"

"I didn't eat anything," Scoops said smirking. "I have been stuck in here all day like a pot of beef stew on simmer." He laughed as he sat back down. "Slow cooking that up like a Crock-Pot."

Riley sat down and pulled the chest of his polo up to cover his mouth. He breathed through the fabric like an air purifier. Sniffing out any scent of laundry detergent or fabric softener, he could trail.

Mrs. Carpenter softly knocked on the door, and the boys froze at the table like park bench sculptures. She entered the room as if it was a greenhouse, but her face instantly screamed outhouse.

The boys sat motionless, their eyes following Miss Carpenter like an old portrait painting. She stopped mid-step, grabbing her long ponytail and placing it under her nose. "You boys can go," she muffled as fast as she could and with expelling as little oxygen as possible. Her eyes started to bulge as she held her breath.

Scoops sat oblivious as if he lacked the sense of smell. He looked at Riley and winked. He couldn't pass on the opportunity to watch her in turmoil. "What do we do with the report?"

She stared at him as if he was a judicial executioner ignoring her plea for life. She knew she had to answer. "Wentworth!" she exhaled and gasped for breath. "Oh my goodness," she cried, clasping her face as she turned and darted out of the room.

By the time the boys had left the library, students had already filed into the hallways. You could hear a pin drop as the students tiptoed down the corridors. At the door to each classroom, a teacher stood, arms crossed supervising as if the kids were death row inmates.

"A waiting room?" Scoops thundered startling the kids next to him. "More like a funeral. What's wrong with these people?"

A group of nearby students looked at him as if he had just ruined their week-long silent retreat on day seven.

"At John Smith High School we respect our fellow students by refraining from unnecessary noise within school property," Riley quoted. His voice riddled with sarcasm.

"Unnecessary noise!" Scoops echoed. "Silence is useless." He walked on his toes, straining to see over the heads of the other students. "Where are those girls?" he asked, growing impatient.

Principal Wentworth was standing in the middle of the hallway like a traffic cop directing students from their lockers to the exits. He glared at each of the students as they passed. Cream stains still visible on his shirt and his buttons by nothing short of a miracle still holding it together.

"Hi, Warden!" Scoops shouted, causing a ripple of turning heads.

The crowd parted as if there was about to be a showdown. A small freckle-faced kid dropped his backpack and ran down the hall out of harm's way.

Principal Wentworth fearfully watched as they approached him. He prepared himself by taking a series of slow deep breaths. As the big man inhaled, he wiped his forehead with the arms of his suit coat.

"You finish your letter, Riley?" his voice trembling as he spoke. "How is the book report coming?"

Scoops shoved the stack of papers against the big man's chest. "Great first day," he said. "What a fantastic start."

They continued to walk right by him.

The startled principal caught the papers just before they dropped and scattered across the hallway. He shook his head in relief, thankful for the brevity of the exchange. As they continued to walk away, he bravely shouted after them. "You boys be back in the study at 8:30 a.m. to continue serving your detention!"

Riley turned and walked backward, "you bet Principal Wentworth. I wouldn't want to miss it for the world!" He spun back around, "by the way. We decided to work together on the report, sir. Two heads are better than one!"

"Have…good night!" Scoops added joyfully waving his arm in the air.

Principal Wentworth shook his head again and turned his attention to the crumpled and damp stack of paper in his hand. Whispers about detention murmured through the hallways of John Smith High School as he began to read Riley's letter.

Dear Mr. Tillweed,

I promise not to change the taps on your water cooler again. It was definitely not worth it. Especially with the time and labour it took to source the required tools and complete the actual prank. Having access to fresh glacier water in our classrooms is such a privilege. As is the genuine care and support you give your students every day. It is unthinkable that I have disrespected you in such a way when you have apparently sacrificed numerous successful, meaningful, and reputable careers because of your passion for educating youth such as myself.

Yours truly,
Riley Kushinski

Principal Wentworth sighed, scrunched the letter into a tight ball in his hands and threw it in a nearby garbage. He hoped to find some redemption in the book report, which surprisingly felt like it was at least twenty pages thick. He read the cover. "Lost, Deserted and Lonely," a book report by Riley and Scoops. Intrigued, he flipped the page to find only a sketch drawing of a map. In the bottom corner of the page was a small note that read.

Dear Ms. Fitz,

We are sorry to hear you have lost your kitten, Mr. Wiggles. Instead of wasting time reading a boring book, we spent the afternoon brainstorming Mr. Wiggle's whereabouts. The following twenty detailed maps include possible hiding places each marked by an X. On a few maps, you will find multiple Xs. When we asked ourselves if we were Mr. Wiggles, where we would be? Sometimes it wasn't so clear so we included all possible destinations a cat might find solace during a trying time such as this. To be mindful of your time, however, we sized each X according to the likelihood Mr. Wiggles is there. We recommend starting with the big Xs.

Cheerio,

Riley and Scoops

5
REFLECTION

When Riley got home, he was surprised to find he had the house to himself. Normally his mom would be there as well as his little sister Charlotte. His father usually got home from the office just in time for dinner and more often than not in time for dessert. His mom rarely left the house except to get groceries, go to the post office and bank. Typical errands that moms do regularly that go unnoticed and unappreciated. He took his coat off, closed the closet door, and hung it on the handle. It fell off as soon as he walked into the kitchen. He immediately smelled something in the oven and was naturally disappointed. Guess we're not going out for dinner tonight, he thought as he went to the oven and peeked in.

"Pork chops," he muttered to himself shaking his head in disapproval. "I haven't eaten all day," he said freely, knowing no one was listening. "Now I get home and have to eat pork chops."

He opened the fridge and stared into it. After about thirty seconds, he noticed a small piece of paper taped to the freezer door and read aloud.

Riley,

Won't be home until suppertime, had to take Charlotte for a haircut.
Love Mom

PS Don't eat anything. We are having pork chops for supper.

"Are those what those are in there?" he asked himself sarcastically. "I thought they were rib-eyes."

He closed the fridge and leaned on the counter. What a great day, he thought as he reflected on the last eight hours, detention, and all. As he concluded it was the first time ever he had a good time at school, he saw the red blinking light on the telephone. Immediately he walked over to push the message button.

"You have one new message," the unrealistically happy recording lady said, "press one if you would like to—" Riley quickly pressed the button as fast as he could to skip right to the message then he heard an all too familiar voice.

"Ms. Fitzpatrick!" Principal Wentworth was yelling. "No, Mr. Wiggles is not in here," he must have realized he was recording. "Oh hi there, Mr. and Mrs. Kushinski," his voice cracking nervously. "This is Principal Wentworth from John Smith High School. I am just calling to talk to you about Riley. I am concerned—"

Riley hit the delete button before Principal Wentworth's message finished.

"Good day for a haircut, Charlotte," he said to himself as he walked into the living room and flopped down on the couch. Riley threw his feet on his mother's coffee table, put his head back, and stared at the ceiling. Before he drifted off to sleep for yet another nap, he thought about how, for the first time, he was excited to go to school the next day.

6
THE STAFF MEETING

At 7:30 a.m. the following day all faculty members were required to attend a last-minute mandatory staff meeting to discuss John Smith High School's most pressing concerns, two students named Riley and Jack. They gathered in the small teachers' lounge surrounding the coffee pot as if it were a campfire. Principal Wentworth fiddled in the corner with a file as if he was running one last time through his speaking notes.

Martin Pripps, the school's gym teacher and second youngest staff member, just slightly older than Miss Carpenter, scratched and rubbed his tired eyes. "What is the problem?" he asked as he examined his colleagues as if they looked different before breakfast. "What monumental catastrophe has occurred that has called us together for such an early morning meeting?" He blew on his steaming coffee. "I accidentally woke up a flock of birds on my bike, and they all laughed at me," he took a sip to build up his audience's anticipation, "they went back to bed after telling me I deserved to have the worm." His chuckled away, but his laughter met nothing but blank stares.

Mr. Tillweed broke the awkward silence. "Not catastrophe, Martin," he said serious as a judge, "catastrophes."

Principal Wentworth cleared his throat. "Ladies and gentlemen, we have a viral infection within the walls of John Smith High School requiring treatment before it spreads any further."

Ms. Fitzpatrick's ears perked up. "Oh dear," she said alarmed. "What is it sir, Smallpox, Polio?"

"No, Ms. Fitzpatrick," Mr. Tillweed snickered. "Those haven't been something to worry about for the past one hundred years."

Miss Carpenter let out a shrill laugh and gently swatted him on the arm of his lab coat.

Ms. Fitzpatrick didn't catch the jab. "Oh thank goodness," she sighed in relief, "those were so terrible."

Tillweed chuckled arrogantly and took a drink of his coffee. He sputtered as the hot liquid burned his already overly sensitive healing lips. "Oh, for heaven's sake," he whimpered.

Miss Carpenter stepped closer, her voice deeply concerned. "Are you alright?"

Tillweed waved her off. "I'm all right," he grumbled, while coffee dripped down his chin.

Principal Wentworth grunted to call the group's attention back to him and continued. "I am talking about disobedience."

The room gasped.

"We have two students who have decided that the rules do not apply to them."

The entire staff was in awe.

"They seem to think that High School is a place to make jokes, to laugh and…" he paused and looked directly at the gym teacher Mr. Pripps, "to have fun."

Pripps looked down at his size twelves. The rest of the staff looked back at the principal as if he had just declared World War 3. The only other sign of life was Mr. Tillweed nodding emphatically in between attempts to blow cool air on his burning lips.

Finally, someone spoke.

"What do we do?" Miss Carpenter asked, her voice trembling.

"We brace ourselves, that is what we do," Principal Wentworth whispered. His response blindsided everyone in the staff room.

"Brace ourselves?" the librarian echoed. "Shouldn't we do something?"

"Yes," Ms. Fitzpatrick screeched as if the sullen meeting had given her flashbacks of the London Blitz. "To the bunkers!" We must get underground now!" She stopped. "Wait, do we have bunkers?" Her eyes widened, "my goodness, I haven't checked the bunkers." She quickly turned and left the room, calling, "Mr. Wiggles! Oh, Mr. Wiggles!"

"Never mind her," Principal Wentworth said, waving his hand. "This is all too much for her."

"Who's Mr. Wiggles?" Ms. Carpenter asked.

Her answer came in the form of a barrage of shrugged shoulders.

Principal Wentworth ignored the question. He turned his gaze to the young gym teacher. "You're young, what do you suggest we do Martin?"

"Well," Mr. Pripps hesitated, appreciating the Principal's observational skills but still wanting to come up with a solution. Unfortunately, he came up short. "Well, I guess I am not really sure."

"We could expel them," Mr. Tillweed suggested.

"I like that," Principal Wentworth approved, and then his eyes narrowed, "no, no, I don't think we can."

Mr. Pripps snapped his fingers. "When I was back in University, I heard of a disciplinary technique where a teacher made disobedient students run laps."

"Laps?" Mr. Tillweed scoffed, "that is a terrible idea."

"Well, what big ideas do you have Tillweed?" retorted Mr. Pripps.

"I could burn holes in them with a Bunsen burner," he said spiritedly, his pupils dilating. "Or mix up a lovely perfume of hydrogen cyanide for them to inhale."

"My goodness Tillweed, how hot was that water?" Principal Wentworth asked nervously as the tall man's sinister smile grew across his face. "I think laps are a much better idea."

Mr. Tillweed protested, "Well, what about something a little bit more painful?"

The Principal shook his head. "I appreciate your creativity, Mr. Tillweed, but I think laps are a good place to start."

A room of stupefied colleagues began to nod their heads in agreement.

Mr. Tillweed didn't hide his displeasure. "What a lame bunch you are," he barked, pointing at each of his peers like they each had personally offended him. "What a blasphemous punishment," he shook his head angrily, "jogging... humph."

He stormed out of the room.

Miss Carpenter looked around the room awkwardly for just a moment, and then quickly followed.

"Don't mind him," Principal Wentworth ordered to the remaining staff, "he didn't have the most fruitful of experiences with our culprits yesterday." He looked at the fit young gym teacher. "Mr. Pripps I will release the boys out of detention today in time for them to join your second-period gym class." His face turned malicious. "Where you will run them until they can no longer walk," his smile grew from ear to ear, "or speak."

Pripps nodded confidently, "leave it to me. I will get this sorted out right away."

7
LOVE AT FIRST SIGHT

Riley and Scoops were ordered to stay in detention until they had finished their book report, but by some miracle, they had qualified for early release. This was a very fortunate turn of events because they were yet to start.

"Sure was nice of Principal Wentworth to let us out early," Riley said cheerfully. "And for gym class," he added slapping Scoops on the shoulder as they left the empty library.

Scoops laughed. "Yeah, I think the big man is really turning a corner. He must have liked your letter of apology to Tillweed."

"Did you bring your gym clothes?" Riley asked. Scoops was wearing the same ripped jeans as the day before but had managed to throw on a loosely fitting bright green t-shirt. He had a generic backpack slung over his right shoulder that carried as if it were empty.

"Yeah, I think so." He flung the bag around to open the zipper and double check.

"You didn't get your locker yet?"

"I went from the Principal's office to detention, remember?"

"Yeah," Riley laughed. "Well, I have to go to my locker and get my gym bag." He tapped his pal on the shoulder, "I will meet you at the gym, ok? You know where it is?"

"I think so. It's that big tall part of the school, isn't it?" Scoops said sarcastically. "High roof, kind of square?"

Riley ignored him. "See you there."

When Riley turned the corner and started down the hallway that led to the gym, he could already hear Scoops calling him.

"Riley!" he squawked, pushing his way through a mass of zombified students. He jumped up and down as he saw Riley approaching. At the apex of each jump, he repeated Riley's name.

Riley could see the excitement all over Scoops' face. "What is it, boy?" he asked, putting his hands on his knees pretending Scoops was his pet dog who had been waiting all day for him to arrive home from work.

Scoops could hardly speak through his excitement. "Who is that?" he stuttered as he pointed at a very attractive brunette and an equally attractive blonde standing by a pair of open lockers with gym bags.

Riley's face lightened, and a smile creviced across his face. "I see you found them." He looked back at Scoops whose tongue was already hanging half out. "Guess who?"

"Them," Scoops sighed. "You have to introduce me." Without hesitation, he grabbed Riley by the arm and dragged him towards the two girls.

"Wait, what are you doing?" Riley cried. "I don't even know them."

It was too late.

"Hi, girls!" Scoops shouted.

The girls looked up startled. Surprised someone was talking in the halls between classes. They looked at each other both unsure if Scoops was addressing them.

They both gave a reserved reply, "hi."

The boys just stood gawking at them.

Finally, Scoops elbowed Riley, who just stared vacantly back at him not sure what to do next. Scoops nudged him again while the girls looked awkwardly at one another.

"Hi, girls," Riley sputtered.

"Hi," the brunette responded again frowning at her friend. "Can we help you?"

The brunette was the taller of the two. She had long, straight dark brown hair she let flow freely down to the middle of her back. She wore a plain white t-shirt with a jean skirt that ended just above her knees.

"We were just wondering how your day was going?"

"Good," the shorter of the two responded brushing away a strand of wavy blonde hair that had fallen in front of her eyes. She parted her hair down the middle with half of it resting down her back while the other half flowed over her soft shoulder and down the front of her black tank top.

Riley couldn't take his eyes off her. "Did you just have gym class?" he asked love-struck, immediately regretting not being able to think of anything better to ask.

The girls looked at each other and then raised their gym bags. "Yeah, what gave that away?" the brunette snubbed.

Realizing how stupid the question was, Riley attempted to recover quickly. "You just looked kind of sweaty."

"Excuse me?" the brunette snapped.

Scoops stepped into to offer his struggling pal some refuge. "Glowing he meant," he offered them his most charming smile, "you girls are glowing."

The blonde smiled while the brunette snarled.

Scoops tried to work some magic. "What was on the schedule today, ping pong, CPR training?" he winked at the tall brunette. "You girls don't look put out at all."

The girls checked out Scoops from head to toe. Then the brunette spoke, "no, we didn't play ping pong."

"Oh," Scoops replied, surprised. "Well, whatever you did is sure working for you." He gave them a thumbs-up. "You two are breathtaking."

The blonde seemed to be admiring Scoops' effort and enjoying the attention. She looked at Riley. "Are you new here?"

"No," Riley admitted, shyly.

Scoops turned to Riley and shot him a disgusted look. "New here? They think you are new here?" He focused his attention back on the girls. "He has been here forever."

The adorable blonde laughed while her friend remained stone-faced and annoyed.

"And you?" The brunette asked in a condemning manner looking down at Scoops as if he were a peasant.

"I am new here," he replied with a smile. He outstretched his hand, "the name is Scoops?"

"Scoops?" she repeated with a snarl, ignoring the gesture to shake hands.

"Yep, that's me," he announced proudly, "pleased to meet you." He had almost forgotten Riley, and the blonde stood next to them. Realizing she wasn't interested in touching him anytime soon, he took his outstretched hand and motioned to Riley. This is my good friend Riley."

"Riley," she repeated sourly again with a similar sneer.

Riley stepped forward and extended his hand. "Pleased to meet you."

She ignored it.

While Riley stood left in the lurch, the cute blonde stepped forward and shook his hand. "I'm Emily," she said with a pleasant smile. "And this is Lisa," she said nodding at the brunette.

Riley shook her hand shyly, grateful she hadn't left him hanging. "It's nice to meet you, Emily." He was starting to perspire. What was just moments seemed to last an eternity. He reminded himself to breathe while Scoops appeared calm and carried on as if he was chatting with long lost friends.

"Lisa, more like Mona Lisa. You ever smile?" Scoops razzed.

"Excuse me!" Lisa fired.

Emily burst out laughing.

Riley cracked an awkward smile, relieved one of them found it funny.

Lisa shoved her gym bag in her locker, grabbed a binder, and slammed the door shut.

As Lisa stormed off down the hall, Emily giggled and quickly stuffed her clothes away too. "Well… it was nice to meet you guys," she said, then smiled sweetly and chased after her friend.

"I love her," Scoops declared.

"Yeah, she is awesome. She is even better looking up close," Riley whispered dreamy-eyed.

Scoops looked at Riley and rolled his eyes. "Up close?" He shook his head as if the thought of Riley never talking to them before had shaken him to the core.

Riley had drifted away to cloud nine and didn't award him any response. "Such pretty eyes…" he fantasized, his words addressed to no one floating off like bubbles in a breeze.

"Yep," Scoops agreed and emitted a long sigh.

"And hair."

"Yep."

"And smile," Riley whispered as the girls turned the corner and were finally out of sight.

"Smile?" Scoops asked. "What smile?"

Riley was baffled. "Who are you talking about?"

"Mona Lisa," Scoops blurted, shocked that they were not talking about the same beautiful girl.

"Lisa?" Riley said repulsed. "Are you kidding?"

"She is beautiful," Scoops closed his eyes, trying to retrieve a mental picture of her. "Such charm, such wit, such personality."

Riley stared at him in awe. "Did you miss that entire conversation?" He scratched his head. "What charm, what wit, what personality?" His voice escalated with each non-existing attribute.

Scoops didn't catch his drift, "She is a real keeper, isn't she?"

Riley shook his head adamantly as if he was yelling no at the top of his lungs. "She is all yours pal. I'm in love with Emily." He slapped him on the shoulder. "Thanks for the introduction buddy."

"No problem," Scoops replied, looking down the hallway as if any minute the girls would return, "anytime."

The boys stood in silence, staring down the corridor. Behind them, two other boys stood antagonistically with their arms crossed. They had heard their entire conversation. The larger of the two cleared his throat. Alarmed, Riley and Scoops turned around.

"How lovely," the smaller of the two said sarcastically, "you boys are in love."

"Indeed, we are," Scoops admitted. "Indeed, we are."

Riley nudged him. "Ahh... Scoops this here is Randle and Todd."

Scoops looked back at Riley as if he was shocked that he didn't know the girls, but knew who these insignificant clowns were. "Well now, that is an introduction," he jeered Riley as he reached his arm out to greet the boys.

"They are Lisa and Emily's boyfriends," Riley mentioned with a nervous smile.

"Oh," Scoops stopped, dropping his hand to his side. "Randle and Todd, you say?"

"I'm Randle, he's Todd," the short unsightly one said pointing at the taller of the two.

"I take it you don't like us talking to your girls?"

"Nope," Todd said, shaking his oversized head.

Scoops rubbed the bridge of his nose as if he was considering it and then replied frankly, "well that just won't do."

Riley began to rock back and forth uncomfortably.

"What do you mean?" Randle grumbled as he stepped forward. His arms still folded. A silver chain swayed back and forth against his tight white t-shirt that did nothing but expose how scrawny he was. He wore overpriced jeans that just barely hung on thanks to the help of a studded black leather belt.

"Well, I am in love," Scoops replied innocently, staring down at Randle's feet examining his leather flip-flops.

"Lisa is my girl," Todd grunted.

"That explains the big smile," Scoops said, laughing.

Todd didn't enjoy the sarcasm. He stepped forward, "listen jokester." Riley and Scoops leaned back. Todd was at least a head taller than both of them and twice as thick which made him three or four times thicker than his skeleton of a buddy. "You're lucky there is no pushing or shoving in the halls." He crossed his arms showing off a pair of giant biceps. "If you want to continue to talk to my girl. You will have to deal with me off school property." He stared hard at Scoops and fiddled with the already rolled up sleeves of his red and blue plaid button-up.

Riley stepped in, "let's go Scoops."

Randle taunted them, "yeah, let's go Scoops." Randle had a small face and a big nose. He laughed as he ran his bony hands through his slicked-back dark hair. He apparently thought he was a lot bigger than he was standing within an arm's length of Todd.

His jeer and weasel face irritated Riley to the bone. The thought of Emily liking him disappointed him. He was starting to worry she was a worse judge of character than Hitler's wife, Eva Braun. He changed his mind about leaving. He knew, but he asked regardless. "And Emily's your girl?" he asked sneering at Randle.

"That is right," he smirked. "Are you in love with her too?"

"Well no, but…" his voice trailed off as he pondered if it was a lie.

"Well no but…" Randle copied again.

"Who is that supposed to be?" Scoops asked, "Is that meant to be him?" He pointed at Riley whose face was getting redder by the minute. "That's a terrible impression."

"Oh yeah," Randle shot back defensively, "you couldn't do any better."

"I think a quadriplegic mime could do better," Scoops stated.

Riley burst out laughing.

"That is funny?" Todd wailed. The jab at his little friend didn't amuse him.

"Pretty funny," Riley answered, laughing. "Kind of like your shorts." He pointed down to Todd's tight white shorts. "You are a little big for those, aren't you?"

Scoops laughed and continued to heckle him. "Yeah, can you bend over in those?"

Todd did everything he could to restrain from hitting them. "I tell you what," he raged. "Why don't we meet after school, and you can really get to know us," he cracked his knuckles, "if you know what I mean."

"I think so," Riley smiled, "just don't think we would find you very interesting."

Scoops nodded. "And what if there is a kids clothing sale on at the mall, wouldn't you want to get there before they sell out of six to nine months?"

"I don't get it," Todd confessed, looking at Randle for help.

"Not surprised," Scoops chuckled.

"They're making fun of your shorts and calling us boring Todd," Randle said, grinding his teeth.

Realizing there was no threat from the boys while on school property, Scoops continued to press. "I think boring is an overstatement."

The warning bell sounded, and Mr. Pripps came out of the gymnasium to find the hallway clear except for the four boys who were still talking. Surprised to see people conversing in the halls, he shouted, "hey, what is going on here?"

"Nothing," Riley answered.

"Absolutely nothing," Scoops reiterated. Staring at Randle and Todd as if they were lulling him off to sleep.

"Todd and Randle go to class." He waved at Riley and Scoops. "You two come with me. You're late."

"This isn't over," Randle growled.

"Yeah this isn't over, stay away from our girls," Todd threatened and stepped forward, so his face was inches away from Scoops' face. "You hear me?"

Mr. Pripps quickly picked up on the hostility and jumped in, "yes, it's over, everybody to class now."

Todd grunted and turned away angrily. Randle did his best to comfort his big pal as they stormed off. "We'll pick this up later Todd," he said loud enough for Riley and Scoops to hear. "Don't worry."

"Well new guy, you are making friends fast," Mr. Pripps said to Scoops. Riley and Scoops followed the young teacher into the gym. By the time they reached the changing room, Scoops had already forgotten about Randle and Todd and was back to daydreaming about his Mona Lisa.

8
MAN DOWN

"We're going outside today," Mr. Pripps announced to the class expecting the chorus of groans that followed. "Track and Field day is tomorrow, so you only have one more chance to practice your event before the big competition."

"Great," Scoops said to Riley. "What event do you do?"

"I don't do events," Riley responded as he hunched down to sit on the dusty gym floor. He had changed into a pair of black shorts and a simple white t-shirt.

Scoops, on the other hand, wore gray shorts with red trim that hung down over his knees. His socks were pulled up, and he wore the same dirty shoes. He pulled his stretched yellow tank top back on his shoulder and laughed, "me neither."

Mr. Pripps walked up to them with his clipboard. He just stared at them in silence until the boys started to feel uncomfortable.

"Yes?" Riley asked, raising his eyebrows.

"Today you gentlemen will be running laps," Mr. Pripps said with a smirk.

"Nope," Riley quickly responded as if there wasn't a chance.

"Yes. Yes, you are," Mr. Pripps insisted, his head bobbing up and down.

"Two things sir," Scoops said. "First, I don't have proper running shoes, and secondly, I am never buying them." He lifted his leg to show the teacher his shoes and almost lost his balance and fell over. "Count me out."

"Gentlemen, it is not my decision," Mr. Pripps replied. "You have two choices, you can either run laps or experience what Mr. Tillweed has planned for you."

"A headache?" Scoops jabbed.

"Boring us to death?" Riley added.

"That's not so bad," Scoops chuckled, "Randle and Todd already tried that."

"Not even close," Mr. Pripps said, shaking his head from side to side. "You don't even want to know."

The boys didn't put up a fight. "You're right, we don't care," Riley said.

Scoops nodded and added casually, "yeah, we'll just wait in here?"

Scoops began to sit down next to Riley and get comfortable. Mr. Pripps took command before he lost their attention. He raised his whistle to his lips and blew it as hard as he could. Both the boys shot up.

"Time to change already, sir?" Riley asked excitedly.

"Yeah that went fast," Scoops said already taking a step toward the change room.

"Track now!" Mr. Pripps shouted.

By the time the boys made it to the track, Scoops was already panting from the short jog. Mr. Pripps and the rest of the class followed behind them and began to fan out to practice individual track and field events. Scoops fell to the lawn just as they reached the starting blocks.

Mr. Pripps started hollering, "start running!"

"How many laps?" Riley yelled back.

Scoops didn't have the breath to speak but managed to push himself up on his knees. He stared across the field of dandelions at the gym teacher with disdain in his eyes.

Mr. Pripps chuckled to himself and shouted back, "Until I tell you to stop!"

Dejected, Scoops struggled to his feet, and the boys started running. Within a few steps, Scoops was almost falling back over. "Arg," he groaned. "I will never make it Riley. I'm going to die."

"Are you kidding?" Riley asked.

"Yeah, running is not my thing," Scoops wheezed.

"Get going!" Pripps called at them as he watched from across the field.

As Riley picked up the pace, Scoops fell to the track as if a sniper hit him and cried out, "I can't make it sorry!" He waved Riley on as if it was okay to leave him behind in enemy territory. "You are going to have to run for both of us, buddy. I just can't. Track isn't my thing."

Riley didn't even turn around or miss a stride. He just laughed and shook his head as he kept running. Behind him, Scoops was already pretending he had passed out hoping Mr. Pripps would let him rest in peace.

Riley had already made about ten laps when Mr. Pripps walked up to Scoops who was sound asleep and snoring in the grass. Flies flew around his head as if he had been dead for hours.

"Mr. Floyd," he said as he walked up.

Scoops didn't budge.

"Mr. Floyd!" he repeated.

Scoops didn't move.

Mr. Pripps nudged him with his toe.

Scoops resurrected. "I'm just too exhausted. I must be dehydrated," he cried. "So much going on sir, so much work with the move and all..." he pretended he passed out again.

It didn't matter. Mr. Pripps had already stopped listening to Scoops. His attention was on Riley who bounded around the track like a greyhound. As he watched him, a smile grew across his face. Such grace, such form, such stamina. As Riley made the turn and headed down the stretch towards him, Mr. Pripps noticed he had yet to break a sweat.

"Good day Mr. Pripps," Riley said as he passed him, his face expressionless.

Scoops rose to his knees to watch Riley. "Pretty good, eh?"

"Magnificent," Mr. Pripps said not taking his eyes of Riley.

Scoops started to babble. "Yeah, track and field is just not my thing, too much running, jumping and throwing stuff. Don't really see the point. Oooh, I can jump this high. Oooh, look at how fast I am. Big deal--all meaningless, really." He started brushing dead grass off his yellow shirt.

Mr. Pripps was not listening to a word he was saying. Riley had already almost made it back to them. He was running at a record-setting pace, and rather than slowing down, he seemed to be picking up speed!

Scoops muttered away as he started to shake grass out of his long hair, "I tried shot put once, well I picked one up, then I put it down. I didn't know it was that heavy."

Suddenly, an angel called out behind him. He turned to see the love of his life and Emily approaching the track. He bolted upright.

Lisa walked up to Mr. Pripps, pretending that she did not notice Scoops was there. "Mr. Pripps, I was thinking about what you said this morning."

Scoops mouth hung open as he stared at her. Time appeared to pass in slow motion.

"I guess I will participate in track," Lisa continued.

"That is great news, Lisa," Mr. Pripps said, he still had not taken his eyes off Riley. Riley was already around the track and approaching them again, and fast.

"Yeah, I think I will try to beat the high jump and discus records…"

Mr. Pripps wasn't listening to Lisa either. He was preoccupied dreaming about being at the next summer Olympics with Riley.

"Hi Emily," Riley said, passing them as if he was taking a light stroll through the park. He picked up the pace once again.

"Faster?" Mr. Pripps mouthed to himself.

"I might even run the 200," Lisa continued.

"That is good," Mr. Pripps droned. In his mind, he was now shoulder-to-shoulder with Riley on the podium belting out the National Anthem.

Scoops didn't miss his chance to jump into the conversation. "What a coincidence, high jump, discus, 200-meters, those are my events." He looked at Lisa with his arms wide open as if she might respond by running into his embrace. "I didn't know you were into track too? What a fluky connection."

Lisa looked at him in disbelief. "You're into track?"

Scoops responded with passion in his voice, "Well, I think it's more like track is into me."

Mr. Pripps scoffed.

Scoops went on, "I was just resting from practicing my sprints." He started to stretch. "You need a training partner?"

Mr. Pripps was starting to get dizzy watching Riley, so he stopped him as he passed. "Riley, that is amazing," he said. "You are like nothing I have ever seen before."

Scoops laughed and looked at Emily. "You might not be Riley's number one fan anymore."

She blushed.

He turned his gaze to Lisa, "how about it Mona Lisa, want to do some sprints, do a little high jumping, discus tossing, pizza eating, movie watching, popcorn sharing—"

"Discus tossing?" she interrupted. "And stop calling me Mona Lisa."

"Hurling? Passing? Shooting?" Scoops misfired, making it completely obvious, he had no idea what he was talking about and knew absolutely nothing about the sport.

"Throwing," she corrected him and crossed her arms.

"Oh yes," Scoops said as if he knew all along. "What about you, Emily? Do you hit the track?"

"The track?" Emily echoed with a smile. "I jog a little, yes."

"Nice," Scoops couldn't hide his excitement. "You and Riley should hit the old dusty trail sometime. Lisa and I would join you, but you know we are more the sprinting type. No time for that slow nonsense. I like to get places you know. Not run around all day. Just get there as fast as possible."

Riley had shaken off Mr. Pripps and caught up with Scoops and the girls.

"Wow," Emily said. "You are a great runner Riley."

"Yeah, you're a real-life Energizer bunny bud," Scoops said, slapping him on the back.

Riley ignored him. "Thanks, Emily, appreciate the compliment."

"Speaking of complements," Scoops said, "we met your boring boyfriends."

The girls looked at each other confused.

"They do not complement you at all."

Lisa still didn't crack a smile. "They're not our boyfriends," she said catching on he meant Randle and Todd. "We're just friends."

"Oh, thank goodness," Scoops said relieved, "I thought you were allergic to personalities or something."

Riley was serious. "That's not what they say."

"Yeah, you better be careful they're super protective," Emily warned.

"Aww, you worried about us?" Scoops flirted.

She blushed, "no, no, I am just saying once you leave school grounds you better watch your backs."

"No worries," Scoops reassured her. "We will stay clear of all libraries, poetry readings, bridge tournaments, and antique auctions for the next few weeks."

"Might even have to skip book club too," Riley added.

"Good idea Riley," Scoops agreed, "and avoid all lawn bowling, tiddlywink competitions, ballets and symphonies as well."

Lisa finally smiled.

"Whoa," Emily and Riley said together in disbelief.

"She smiles," Scoops said slack-jawed, "I didn't think it was possible."

"Come on," Lisa protested, "what did you think I was, completely miserable?"

"No," Scoops said, trying to regain his composure, "I just didn't think it was possible."

"What?" Lisa was getting agitated. "You thought I was incapable of having fun and joking around?"

"No," Scoops said, "that you could look even more beautiful."

Lisa instantly melted. She blushed and didn't know what to say.

Emily was smiling too. "We better get back to class, Lisa."

"Alright," Lisa replied as she ran her fingers through her long dark hair. She smiled again, and they all started walking back to the school.

Inside the school doors, Randle and Todd stood watching them with their hands on their hips.

9
IT'S JUST CHEMISTRY

"Well this won't be awkward at all," Riley said as he and Scoops made their way to third block, Mr. Tillweed's science class.

"I still can't believe we are in this class together, buddy," Scoops said. "I just can't believe it."

"Yeah, it doesn't seem like the wisest of decisions Principal Wentworth has made. Almost worse than putting on shoes that didn't match yesterday."

"Nope, sure doesn't," Scoops agreed. "Hey, we should be lab partners."

As they walked into the science room, Mr. Tillweed's jaw stiffened.

"Good afternoon, Mr. Tillweed," the boys said politely.

"Good afternoon," he replied, already suspicious of what they were going to do next.

"How is your day going?" Scoops asked courteously.

"Fine," Mr. Tillweed replied. He turned his head away, revealing his anxiety. "And yours?"

"It's just great sir, thanks for asking." Scoops plopped down into an empty desk. "Just glad to be out of the library and excited to learn sir."

Mr. Tillweed didn't give them the benefit of the doubt. "Okay, what are you guys up to?"

Riley was making his way over to the water cooler. "What do you mean, sir?" He asked, innocently. "I think Scoops is just being friendly."

"I see."

"Yep, just being friendly is all," Scoops seconded.

Mr. Tillweed noticed Riley at the water cooler and sprung to action, "step away from the cooler Mr. Kushinski, Mr. Wentworth revoked your water cooler privileges, remember?"

"But," Riley begged, "I am thirsty, sir."

"I will get you one bud," Scoops said, jumping out of his seat to come to his friend's aid. "Riley's been running like the wind all day sir, nothing but laps for this poor guy."

"Both of you sit down now," he grumbled.

Riley sighed and sat down next to Scoops.

To spite them, Mr. Tillweed shuffled his way over to the cooler, carefully took his coffee mug and poured a bit of cold water into it. He raised it to his lips slowly and stopped before they touched the ceramic, almost as if he was testing if there was heat coming off the water.

Riley grimaced as he tilted the cup.

Mr. Tillweed stopped.

Riley smiled, and Mr. Tillweed knew he was playing him. He took a swig of cold water then addressed the whole class. "Today we will learn about —" a soft knock on the door interrupted him.

He rested his mug on his desk and made his way to the door. "Excuse me," he apologized to the class. He then opened the door a crack. The classroom could hear him whispering. "Oh, hi Miss Carpenter, how can I help you?" Her voice was inaudible. "Sure, I can help." Mr. Tillweed turned back to face the class. "Turn to chapter four and begin reading. I will be right back." He closed the door behind him to the ruffling of turning pages.

"What is with those two?" Scoops asked. "Somebody file a book wrong and she called in a search party?"

The teachers were not fooling Riley. "I think Mr. Tillweed wants to check her out of the library."

"Sick," Scoops said, scrunching his face. He got up and walked to the cooler. He turned and scanned the class. Every student was face deep in chapter four. "How cooperative," he whispered to Riley as he turned the water cooler around and quickly popped off the back panel.

"What are you doing?" Riley gasped.

"There is no point starting something Riley if you don't intend to finish it." The mechanics of the cooler were not hard to figure out. Two small rubber tubes connected the water to the taps. It was almost too simple to pop the tubes off and switch them.

Riley shook his head, disappointed that he had taken the time to unscrew the taps when a quick switcheroo would have sufficed. Scoops had changed the tubes, popped the panel back on, and sat back down in less than a minute.

When Mr. Tillweed came back into the room a few minutes later, he had a spring in his step and a twinkle in his eye. Riley and Scoops watched him as he sat down and tapped his fingers on his desk calendar as if he was drumming an up-tempo beat. Unbeknownst to him, he had a small smear of cherry red lipstick on his lips.

"Um, excuse me, Mr. Tillweed," Riley whispered, trying to get his attention.

Mr. Tillweed threw his head back, annoyed. "What is it, Riley?"

"Did you just have a popsicle or something?" He knew it was Miss Carpenter's lipstick.

Scoops didn't want to miss out, "I love popsicles, especially red ones, what was it? Cherry?"

Mr. Tillweed instantly became flustered and his face turned red from embarrassment. He bolted out of his chair, grabbed some tissues off his desk and quickly walked to the water cooler. He crumpled up the tissue and placed it under the cold waterspout. Scoops couldn't have drawn it up any better. Hot water started to pour out of the tap onto the squashed tissue. It took a few seconds for the pain to set in. Mr. Tillweed shrieked and threw the tissue against the wall as fast as he could. "Kushinski!" he screamed. He blew on his hands, "new kid, office now!"

"Your office looks great Principal Wentworth," Scoops said, examining it as if he was a health inspector as Mr. Tillweed led him and Riley into Principal Wentworth's office for their second visit in two days. It looked the same as it did the previous day.

73

"Where is Ms. Fitz?" Riley asked, concerned. He wasn't aware she had been missing since the impromptu morning staff meeting.

"Never mind," Principal Wentworth barked, he was not interested in exchanging pleasantries. "What is it now, Mr. Tillweed?"

"They are up to their old tricks already," Mr. Tillweed growled.

Principal Wentworth frowned. "The water cooler again?"

"Yes," he held up his hand to show the principal how red it was.

"For heaven's sake… Ms. Fitzpatrick!" Principal Wentworth shouted, but immediately remembered she was missing in action. He picked up the phone on his desk and dialed an extension. "Yes, Mr. Pripps, can you join us in my office, please. Yes now. I don't care, bye." His face was red, and he looked like he was going to have a heart attack.

"It seems like every time we meet you, Mr. Wentworth, you are having a real downer of a day," Scoops said cheerfully.

Principal Wentworth didn't reply. Instead, he just raised a crumpled-up bundle of tissue to his forehead and mopped up the sweat.

"Speaking of wiping things off," Riley commented. "Did you get all that cherry popsicle off your lips, Mr. Tillweed?"

Mr. Tillweed snorted, "why you…"

"Popsicle?" Principle Wentworth asked as if the word was a stimulus and he suddenly craved one.

Mr. Tillweed just shook his head from side to side.

"Well, what was it Mr. T?" Riley prodded, "lipstick or something?"

Mr. Tillweed quickly responded to steer the conversation, "it was a Firecracker."

"I think a Firecracker is a popsicle," Scoops pointed out. "They call them Turbo Rockets too I think."

"I agree. Those are those red, white, and blue ones, aren't they?" Riley asked.

"Yep, they're pretty tasty," Scoops added. "Don't think Mr. Tillweed made it to the white part though."

"Yeah, too bad. I like the white part."

"Me too."

"What is your favorite part?" Riley asked Scoops.

"Blue I think, but I can't really remember. Maybe Mr. Tillweed has more?"

Mr. Tillweed grumbled, "no, I don't have any popsicles."

"I think we already got to the bottom of that. Firecrackers are popsicles."

"Yeah," Riley confirmed, "if you have one of those that would be great."

"Or maybe Miss Carpenter has one," Scoops suggested.

Mr. Tillweed clenched his fists and locked his knees. "You two are despicable. You don't care about anything or anybody. You probably don't even know what you want to be when you graduate, do you?"

Scoops quickly replied. "Yes, sir, I want to be what you wanted to be," he jabbed. "Don't worry, sir. I won't give up and make sure my dreams come true for both of us. You can live vicariously through me."

Mr. Tillweed was just about to leap across the small office and tackle Scoops, but Mr. Pripps knocked on the door, averting the crisis.

"Come in, Mr. Pripps," Principal Wentworth said, thankful for the interruption.

"How are you feeling, Riley?" Mr. Pripps asked, tapping him on the shoulder.

Scoops spoke up as if he was Riley's sports agent. "He is doing great, thanks Pripps. Heck of a practice today, I think he will be ready for the big day."

"That is great, just great," Mr. Pripps replied. "What is this all about?" he asked as he looked at Principal Wentworth and Mr. Tillweed.

"How did running laps work out today, Mr. Pripps?" Wentworth asked with a sneer. "Get to the bottom of our little problem at all?"

"Absolutely sir, you should see this kid run. We finally have someone at this school that can actually compete."

"Not that problem, Mr. Pripps!" Wentworth replied angrily.

"Then what are you talking about?" Mr. Pripps suddenly remembered. "Oh," he mumbled. "What did they do now?"

Mr. Tillweed couldn't hold back. "They fiddled with my cooler again."

"Geez, Mr. Tillweed," Mr. Pripps scoffed, "get a water bottle or thermos like the rest of us and get over it."

"You get a water bottle!" Mr. Tillweed shot back.

"I do have one, a glass one, free of BPA's and other cancerous toxins!"

"You're a cancerous toxin!" Mr. Tillweed shouted.

"Silence, the both of you," Principal Wentworth directed as he struggled to his feet. "What kind of example are you setting?"

"Couldn't agree more sir," Riley chimed in, "I am at a loss these days, just not sure where to turn for role models anymore, first Adam and Eve, now Mr. Tillweed?"

"Cram it Kushinski!" Mr. Wentworth scolded. "I am too tired for all of this." He gasped for breath, pulling at his belt as if another inch would relieve him of all the stress and anxiety they were causing him. "I am suspending you two for the rest of the week."

"Rest of the week?" Scoops, Riley, and Mr. Pripps chorused.

Mr. Pripps advocated on Riley's behalf. "He can't be suspended. He needs to run tomorrow."

"Yeah, I can't be suspended either, sir," Scoops complained, "I have to jump things and toss the discus and stuff."

The room ignored him. All eyes focused on Riley, who was silently hoping the suspension would stand, and he wouldn't have to participate in the boring race. "I don't mind. I don't have to run."

"Suspended," Mr. Tillweed steamed. "That is it? What about my hand? My lips?"

Principal Wentworth stood behind his desk, fiddling with his old gold watch. "I can't handle this anymore." He unbuttoned his cuffs and started rolling up his sleeves. I have to conduct the Bridgeport Orchestra this Saturday and can't afford any more distractions."

The room went deathly quiet, a round of frowns wrinkled through the room.

"Bridgeport Orchestra?" Mr. Tillweed repeated, breaking the silence.

"Don't want to miss that," Scoops joked. He leaned forward, analyzing a picture on the desk of the Principal in action.

Everybody chuckled, except the Principal.

"That is it!" Principal Wentworth roared. He slammed his fists on his desk again and bolted upright. His shirt finally tore at the seams. Buttons flew across the room like shrapnel from a grenade. Everyone ducked and covered. Principal Wentworth stood, his shirt ripped open, exposing a white undershirt camouflaged with yellow sweat stains. "Kushinski! Floyd!" he shouted as he took his dress shirt off and hurled it to the floor, "back to the library, now!"

"For how long?" Mr. Pripps intervened.

Principal Wentworth sent him daggers but then saw Riley, who looked too content with the idea of detention. He changed his mind.

"Riley," the big man said, pointing a chubby finger in his face, "you will run tomorrow."

Riley slumped in his chair.

"Yes!" Mr. Pripps clapped and pumped his fist.

Principal Wentworth whipped his pen at him. "And if he loses you better look for another job, Mr. Pripps! And far from Bridgeport!"

"Yeah," Mr. Tillweed scowled, unhappy with the proceedings, "far away Pripps."

"And you!" Principal Wentworth yelled at Mr. Tillweed. His comment was a red cape drawing the raging bull's anger. He continued to charge, "No more…" he exploded, "no more popsicles!"

The room was silent.

Until Scoops chimed in softly as if on cue, "or Firecrackers."

Mr. Tillweed looked as though he was about to blow fire.

Scoops pressed the Principal. "What about me, sir, I have a lot of events too. Jump high, discus, kind of a big deal to me."

"Absolutely not!" he shouted. "You will stay in detention."

"Ahh, no way," Scoops whined. "I have to sir. I'm kind of a big deal."

The Principal shook his head as he picked up his baton and started polishing it with a rag as if it was his mechanism for collecting himself and returning to a positive mental state. "No."

Scoops wasn't going to give up. He knew he could leverage Mr. Tillweed's romantic scandal. He looked at the tall man who was still staring at him as if he was lost in his own mind planning the perfect murder. Scoops gently put his forefinger to his lips and pretended to put on lipstick. Scoops subtle action brought Mr. Tillweed back from the evidence board and into reality. He looked like he was about to strike Scoops, but wisely, he restrained. He had to keep his relationship from Principal Wentworth.

"Mr. Wentworth," he advised, "with your big event Saturday night, perhaps you should pull Scoops out of detention tomorrow and let him participate."

Scoops sat back in his chair, enjoying watching his new defense attorney at work. "Perhaps he can help us win for once. And if he is in the field, you won't have to keep an eye on him all day in detention." He looked at Scoops who had stopped pretending to put on lipstick. "Then you can focus on your concert."

"Symphony," Principal Wentworth corrected him. He breathed on his baton to moisten it and softly wiped it off. "Fine," he said, holding the baton up to the light to check for smudges.

"Yeah!" Scoops yelped and stood up, holding his hand out to high-five Mr. Tillweed.

Mr. Tillweed held up his iced hand.

Scoops shrugged and winked. "Air five?"

Satisfied that his baton was clean, and feeling a lot more relaxed, Principal Wentworth gently set the baton on his desk. "Everybody out," he instructed calmly.

The room began to clear.

Riley stood from his chair, still not satisfied with his sentence. He picked up Principal Wentworth's spotless baton and rolled it between his fingers as if it were a scroll.

Principal Wentworth gasped as he held it up to the light.

"Looks good sir," Riley said, nodding in approval.

Principal Wentworth reached forward to snatch the baton out of Riley's hand, slamming his belly into the edge of his desk. "Give me that!" he roared. "And get out of my office!"

Riley smiled as he hurried out to catch up with Scoops.

Behind him, Principal Wentworth had restarted his self-regulation routine and was madly scrubbing his baton.

10
FIRST IMPRESSIONS

When the dismissal bell rang, the boys left detention without waiting for a staff member to come and let them out. Principal Wentworth had long since given up on the book report, so there was nothing to hand in. When they walked out of the school's front entrance, Lisa and Emily were just jumping into the back of a rare brand new convertible Lamborghini sedan. The sun glistened off its red paint and it shined as if it had never left the showroom. Riley and Scoops didn't notice the car. Their focus was on the girls. When they saw them, they ran down the steps and up to student pick-up area calling for them to wait. The driver wore a dark black suit with dark shades to match his thick goatee. As they approached, they could hear classical music blasting out of the car stereo.

"Hi girls," Scoops said as they approached. As they rushed to catch them, the boys had forgotten what they wanted to say.

"Hi," Emily responded.

Lisa said nothing.

The man in the front seat turned his head slowly, lowered his glasses with his left hand to look Riley and Scoops over.

"Good afternoon," Riley said politely.

"Yes?" was his only response. He looked annoyed that he had to communicate with two adolescents. He turned down the volume and then proceeded to brush a small piece of fuzz off the plush leather passenger seat with the back of his fingers.

Riley got the hint the man was not interested in any social interaction of any kind. "We just wanted to say bye to our friends."

"Bye, guys," Emily said. "This is Lisa's dad, Emilio."

Scoops had finally noticed the car. "Pleasure, Emilio," he sang cheerfully. "Really like your car, sir."

"Dr. Fiore," he hissed back at Scoops.

"Sorry sir," Scoops said apologetically, "sounds Italian."

Lisa's father let out a suppressive sigh and pushed his shades back up slowly, "does it?"

Scoops looked genuinely offended by the man's demeanor but being that this was his future father-in-law he wasn't going to give up until he had won him over. "How many horses you got under the hood?" he asked, winking at the girls in the back seat.

Dr. Fiore turned slowly to look at him. As he did, he slowly tapped his steering wheel as if he was waiting for a green flag to drop. He replied nonchalantly. "She's got a V10," he gave Scoops and Riley an arrogant half smile, "roughly 600 bulls are charging under the hood."

"Are there?" Scoops replied, nodding as if he knew what any of that information meant.

The dark-haired man continued, "Yeah, she really purrs," he paused and looked smugly at Scoops, "and when I want her to, she roars."

Scoops rolled his eyes, "really?"

Riley looked at him knowing Scoops had tossed in the towel. He braced himself as Scoops continued.

"With all those bulls under the hood, I would have thought it snorted."

Everyone laughed except Dr. Fiore, who was not enjoying Scoops repartee. "Are we done?" he snarled back at Scoops.

Scoops quickly turned his attention to Lisa before her dad could throw the car into gear and speed off. "So Lisa, you want to practice tonight for tomorrow?"

"Um, well—" she started, but her father cut her off.

"Practice, what do you need to practice?" he asked Scoops eyeing him from top to bottom as if he couldn't believe he had any athletic prowess whatsoever.

"Track and field sir," Scoops replied as confident as a world champion, "big meet tomorrow, and I thought I could help her get ready?"

The man scoffed. "It looks like the only thing you could help my daughter with is flunking her way out of college."

He cackled to himself.

Riley had admired Scoops attempt and for a short time, his restraint. Uh-oh, he thought as he and Emily's eyes locked, they both could sense the storm that was about to hit.

"I am not going to college, sir," Scoops said matter-of-factly.

The man responded cynically, "big surprise there."

"Yep," Scoops said, "straight to work for me, going to have to make the big bucks."

"Why is that?" Lisa's dad asked as he calmly rubbed the outline of the Lamborghini bull on his steering wheel with the tip of his middle finger like it was braille.

"Well," Scoops orated, "Lisa and I are getting married." His face was deadly serious. "Going to need to look after the family, you're never too young to fall in love, sir."

"Scoops," Lisa objected, wanting to put an end to the confrontation.

"Scoops?" her dad repeated, rolling his eyes in disapproval, paying no attention to the marriage commentary. "What kind of name is that?"

Scoops dodged the question and leaned forward, putting his arms on the door of the sports car. He wasn't about to back down, especially not in front of Lisa. "Dr. Fiore," he said as pompous as he could, "what kind of doctor is Dr. Fiore?"

Emilio smirked. "I am a psychiatrist."

"I see," Scoops replied boldly, "so not a real doctor."

Dr. Fiore shifted in his seat. He turned to face Scoops. "I am a physician you ignoramus. I help many people every day."

"How is that?" Scoops replied sarcastically, "teaching them rudimentary social etiquette?"

Dr. Fiore scoffed, "I conduct clinical assessments by thorough mental status examinations and other processes you wouldn't understand."

Scoops leaned forward so he could stare in Dr. Fiore's dark sunglasses, "well then, what am I thinking?"

"I am not a psychic!" Dr. Fiore shot back angrily. "I'm a psychiatrist. I get as deep as I can into the brains of my patients to diagnose and treat their mental disorders."

Riley liked where the conversation was headed and joined in. "Good thing you're not a proctologist."

Emily giggled and quickly covered her mouth so Dr. Fiore didn't notice.

Dr. Fiore had had enough. "It was a pleasure to meet you," he said sarcastically. "If you will excuse us, we have lives to enjoy."

As Dr. Fiore and the girls peeled out of the parking lot, Riley tried to comfort his friend. "Well, that was pleasant."

"Yeah," Scoops replied solemnly, "I hope I don't pull his name in the Christmas gift exchange."

Riley laughed and put his arm around him. He could tell Scoops already regretted his first impression. "Want to come over?" Riley asked, shaking him gently. "I just live a few blocks from here."

"Sure," Scoops answered, still tossing the conversation with Lisa's father around in his head. "How did that go off the rails so fast?"

"He was a jerk," Riley answered. "It wasn't your fault."

"There is a lot of those around here isn't there?" he said soberly.

Riley tried to cheer Scoops up. "You know, I just fired my psychic."

"Oh yeah, why is that?"

"I went to see her, and she told me she wasn't expecting me, so I knew she wasn't any good."

"Good one," Scoops let out a half smile.

As they started down the sidewalk towards Riley's house, a big Buick sedan rolled up beside them. Randle hung his arm out of the window as if he was a long-haul truck driver. His pale, hairless arm reflecting more sunlight than the chrome trim that outlined the car windows.

"Saw you talking to our girls again," he snarled.

"Your girls?" Scoops shot back aggressively. He was close to losing his cool.

Riley could sense Scoops dispirited mood and tried to uplift him with some more quick wit. "Hi, Randle," Riley said, leaning down, looking past him at Todd. "Taking your escort home?"

Todd grumbled.

"I see you are walking home?" Randle rebutted.

The two chuckled.

"Why, you want us to give us a ride?" Riley asked. "Sorry, can't do, that boat would make me seasick. Where do all the rowers fit in that old galley anyway?"

Randle and Todd looked at each other searching for a clue.

Riley threw them a lifebuoy. "Ship," he said, shaking his head.

"Hysterical," Randle said, wiping his nose with his finger. He put Scoops back into his sights. "Heard you are going to try your luck with discus and high jump? Those are Todd's events," he warned.

Scoops was still visibly upset. "Todd owns those events too, does he?" He kicked at some weeds growing out of a crack in the sidewalk, "as well as the girls?"

"Todd is quite the tycoon, what software do you use to keep inventory?" Riley chimed in. "Must be hard on your ego hey Randle, Todd got all the height, muscles, business acumen. He pretty much owns everything. You really drew the short straw, didn't you?"

"Short everything," Scoops piled on, "short spine, short neck, and short legs, short—"

Riley interrupted. "Is that why you have such a long car, Randle?"

Randle snarled and released the brake. The car lurched forward, and Randle pushed the brake pedal back to the floor, jerking them forward in their seats. Todd nearly hit his head against the dashboard.

"Careful there," Riley advised. "You almost knocked the champ out before his big day."

Randle and Todd were ready to get out of the car and pound Riley and Scoops but were surrounded by teachers and parents.

Todd hammered his fist against the glove compartment in frustration.

"You leave Lisa and Emily alone, you hear," Randle shot. "If we catch you talking to them again, you're dead."

"That's rude," Riley said calmly.

Scoops went into a rant. "Yeah, who do you guys think you are anyway, King Herod, ready to execute anyone who might get in your way?"

Riley wasn't going to let Randle and Todd keep him away from Emily. "The girls have minds of their own," his voice serious as a priest in a confessional, "they are not your property. They can choose for themselves."

"Hah!" Randle scoffed. "Is that so? Well, we will see about that."

He sped off, causing Todd's head to snap back against his headrest. Black smoke poured out of the old Buick's exhaust pipe, leaving Riley and Scoops in a giant cloud of fumes.

Scoops coughed and wafted his hand in front of his face. "What a joke. Who are these people?"

Riley looked at Scoops and sympathized as he saw the look of discouragement return to his face. It was evident that the constant shelling of hostility was starting to chink his armor. "Come on, Scoops," he said warmly, "let's go eat, my mom will have a good dinner on and will want you to join us."

When Scoops saw Riley's home, his jaw dropped. It was a large beautiful brick house with twin dormer windows over an expansive white-columned porch. Two colourful flower baskets hung from the porch roof on each side of a large white entry door. On the east side of the house, there was a small den, and to the west a large two-door garage. As they walked in, they could smell a roast in the oven. Scoops nostrils flared, and his eyes lit up.

"Supper smells good mom!" Riley shouted into the kitchen.

"Oh, hi," she replied. Riley's voice had startled her. She walked to the front entrance to welcome him home. As she walked into the room wiping her hands on her apron, she saw Scoops and smiled cheerfully.

"Good, you're home," she said as she studied the strange tall blonde in her entryway.

"This is Jack. He just moved to Bridgeport."

"Scoops," Scoops corrected Riley.

"Well, nice to meet you," she greeted, reaching out to shake his hand.

Scoops shook her hand ever so gently.

"Can you stay for dinner?" she asked.

"Yes, thank you. I would love that."

As Scoops continued to surprise Riley with his good manners, his father came bursting in from the garage with his briefcase in hand.

"Honey, I am home," he sang as if he was reenacting an old scene from a fifties movie.

Riley's mom laughed as if it was the first time she had seen him do it.

"He does that every day," Riley said as he rolled his eyes.

"Great timing," Mrs. Kushinski said. "Riley and his new friend just got home, and he is going to join us."

"Great news," Riley's dad said. He looked delighted as he walked up to Scoops. "Welcome son, glad to have you."

"Thank you, sir," Scoops replied politely. "Appreciate you having me."

"Where you from?" Riley's father asked, taking off his shoes.

Scoops dodged around the question. "We just moved here, sir."

Riley's dad frowned, "I know, where from?"

They all began to funnel into the kitchen.

Riley jumped into the conversation. "His dad's a lawyer like you, dad. And guess what?"

"What's that?" he asked, giving Riley's mom a kiss on the cheek as she drained the potatoes. He walked to the fridge, pulled out the milk and butter, and began adding them to the big pot.

"He works at your office. What a coincidence, huh?"

Mr. Kushinski frowned again. He looked at Scoops, who quickly turned away. "Anything I can help with Mrs. Kushinski?" Scoops asked.

"Sure Scoops, can you please make a jug of ice water. I think that is all that is left," Mrs. Kushinksi said and looked around the kitchen. "Just use the water and ice from the dispenser on the fridge."

She addressed Riley, "can you call your sister, please?"

"Scoops?" Mr. Kushinski whispered to himself as he washed his hands in the kitchen sink.

Riley's mom saw him and swatted at him with an oven mitt, "don't do that here," she scolded.

Scoops smiled as he watched them from the fridge, waiting for the pitcher to fill.

"Relax," Mr. Kushinski said as he tickled her. As she giggled, he noticed a look of grief sweep over Scoops' face. While Mr. Kushinski mashed the potatoes, Scoops looked out the back window as if lost in a distant memory.

"Let's eat," Mr. Kushinski said. "I think we're ready."

Riley's sister skipped into the kitchen, singing at the top of her lungs. As soon as she saw Scoops, she panicked and ran out of the room right back into Riley, who followed her down the hallway. "Who is that?" she asked.

"That is my friend, Jack," Riley replied as if it was inconsequential.

"I will be right back," she called as she ran back up the stairs to the bathroom.

"What's she doing now?" Mr. Kushinski asked as Riley walked back into the kitchen.

"Who knows," Riley replied as he sat down at the table.

Scoops put the water jug on the table and sat down beside him.

Riley's mom tapped Mr. Kushinski. When he looked back at her, she pointed to her face and made a small circular motion. "Make-up," she whispered. She shot a glance at Scoops. "He's cute."

"Oh geez," Mr. Kushinski replied, rolling his eyes. "Charlotte!" he shouted, "come for supper now!"

The four who remained in the kitchen sat down at the table. Finally, after a couple of minutes, Charlotte made her way nervously to the table.

"Hi," she said shyly to Scoops.

"Thank you for gracing us with your presence," Mr. Kushinski said impatiently. "Is it ok if we eat now?"

"Sorry dad, I forgot something," she lied.

Riley finally clued into what was happening. He kicked Charlotte under the table, "what, that you're ten?"

"Riley," Mrs. Kushinski defended her. "Let's give thanks. Supper is getting cold."

Mr. Kushinski set his elbows on the table and folded his hands. "Scoops, would you like to say grace?"

"I can, dad," Riley said quickly to pinch hit for his friend.

"That's alright Riley, I got this," Scoops replied confidently.

Scoops clasped his hands and closed his eyes. Riley left one eye open, fearing for the worst.

"Thank you, Lord, for this excellent food, for caring friends, family, and the many blessings we have in our lives. We pray for those less fortunate and pray that you comfort them in time of need. Thank you, Father," he lifted his head and opened his eyes, "Amen."

Riley was shocked. Scoops was a real pro.

"Thank you, Scoops," Riley's mom said. "What a wonderful blessing."

"Yeah," Charlotte breathed, as she stared across the table gawking at Scoops.

"Pass the potatoes, Charlotte," Riley yelled and tossed a bun at her.

"This looks excellent, Mrs. Kushinski," Scoops said. "My mom hasn't made a meal like this for a long time."

Mrs. Kushinski responded, "thanks, Scoops, appreciate—" she jumped up. "Oh, my goodness, my salad."

They all laughed as she ran to the fridge to get the forgotten greens.

"Almost forgot," she chuckled as she sat back down. "Speaking of forgetting," she continued. "Riley, there was a message from Principal Wentworth today saying he called yesterday, but I hadn't got back to him."

Riley stopped chewing.

"Did you forget to pass a message on to me?"

Mr. Kushinski slapped a spoonful of mashed potatoes on his plate, his eyes darting back and forth between Riley and his mother.

"Nope," Riley lied.

"How about you Scoops? Know what that might be about?" she tested.

"Yep," Scoops replied.

"You do?" She asked, surprised.

Riley stared at Scoops as if he was going impale him with the butter knife.

"Routine call," Scoops explained.

Riley breathed a sigh of relief, knowing the friend he knew was back.

Scoops carried on, "just calling all the parents to let them know about track and field day."

"Track and field?" Mr. Kushinski ears perked up. "I love track and field day."

"Probably why they were calling, sir," Scoops said nodding. "Making sure you don't miss it."

"When is it?" Mr. Kushinski asked Scoops.

"Tomorrow, sir."

Riley shook his head. "Ah shucks, you have to work dad. Don't know why they don't have these on the weekends."

"I can probably get away," Mr. Kushinski said. "What event are you doing, Riley? When I was young, I was a runner."

"Could run like the wind your father," Mrs. Kushinski reminisced.

Scoops nodded his head up and down as if he just received super galactic oneness. "Ah," he whispered. "That makes a lot of sense. Riley is a really good runner."

Mr. Kushinski asked proudly, "What are you running, son?"

"The opposite way of the track," Riley replied as he shoved another helping of potatoes into his mouth.

Mr. Kushinski looked disappointed.

"Do you run too, Scoops?" Charlotte asked. She hadn't touched her food yet.

"Nope, not me." Scoops crammed a slab of roast beef in his mouth. "I'm not a runner at all. I don't even really enjoy walking all that much."

"Scoops would only use a Stairmaster if it had a down setting," Riley joked.

"Eat up Charlotte," Mrs. Kushinski said.

"I'm not hungry," she said. She didn't dare to take her eyes off their dinner guest.

Mr. Kushinski steered the conversation back to track and field. "Well, I would like to come to watch you, son," he wiped his face with a napkin. "What time?"

Scoops answered for Riley. "He will be running all day, sir. He doesn't stop." He took a big bite out of an overly buttered bun. "Want to watch me too?" he asked.

"I do," Charlotte said. A bit too loud.

"Thanks, Charlotte," Scoops said with a big wink. Charlotte almost passed out into the gravy.

"What events are you in…" Mr. Kushinski had to pause to remember his odd name, "Scoops?"

"Jump rope, discus and the 200 sprint, sir."

"Jump rope?" Mr. Kushinski replied, confused. "That is in track and field now?"

"I jump rope," Charlotte professed.

Riley set them straight. "High jump."

"Oh yeah, high jump," Scoops said, and spooned the last of his potatoes into his mouth.

Mr. Kushinski smiled and a look of disappointment fell across Charlotte's face.

Scoops pushed his plate away and wiped his lips. "That was terrific."

"You're terrific," Charlotte drooled.

"Charlotte, take the dishes to the sink," her mom demanded.

The boys helped clear the table and then went outside to the backyard. They sat on the edge of the deck and watched the sun start to set.

"Thanks for having me over, Riley," Scoops said. "You have a really nice family?"

"Riley!" His mother called from inside the house. "Can you help your sister, please?"

Riley looked at Scoops and groaned. As he stood up, he patted him on the shoulder, "anytime, buddy."

Riley passed his father at the patio doors. "Nice night," Mr. Kushinski said as he came outside. It had gone completely dark within a few minutes. "Mind if I join you?" he asked Scoops.

Scoops just nodded.

Mr. Kushinski stood at the patio table and opened a bottle of wine. After he had poured a glass, he sat down on the deck next to Scoops. "So, your father is a lawyer?"

"No, Mr. Kushinski," Scoops admitted, expecting to have another hearty adult to teenager one-sided chat.

"Call me John," Mr. Kushinski said.

"Mr. Kushinski was your father?"

Mr. Kushinski laughed, "that old chestnut, hey?" He smiled at Scoops warmly. "What does your father actually do?"

Scoops stared at his shoes. They were old and worn, and pieces of white artificial leather flaked off them as he rubbed them together.

"He worked for our municipality," Scoops said.

"What does he do now?"

Scoops mood immediately turned very somber. "He passed on, sir."

Scoops' answer was unexpected. Mr. Kushinski thought Scoops dad might have left him and his mother, or hoped Scoops was only ashamed of his occupation. "I am sorry son, I didn't know."

"No, that is okay." Scoops smiled at him to make sure he didn't feel bad. "No one does."

Mr. Kushinski stared into the dark, "no one?"

"Yes, and please don't tell?"

"Why?" Mr. Kushinski whispered, looking over his shoulder as if Riley was about to come back outside at any moment.

Scoops shrugged, "I just don't want to bum him out, you know? It's no big deal. We moved here to move on, not dwell in the past."

"I'm sorry Scoops, when did you lose him?"

"Last month."

"Last month?" Mr. Kushinski was so surprised he almost poured wine down the front of his shirt. "Oh, Scoops, I'm sorry."

Scoops put on his bravest smile, "No worries. No bad memories just great times." He tapped Mr. Kushinski on the leg. "Tell me about your running days."

Mr. Kushinski laughed. "They were something."

"Really?"

"No," he replied chuckling. "All bad memories, no good times."

They both laughed.

"Why do you want Riley to run?" Scoops asked.

"Sounds like something a dad should want, doesn't it?" he set his glass down and put his hands on his knees. "Can you keep a secret too?"

Scoops rubbed his shoes together. "Yep."

"I don't really care."

They laughed again.

"Listen," Mr. Kushinski said. He started to slide off the deck onto the lawn. "I think I have something you might like. I will be right back."

As soon as he went into the house, Riley came back out as if they were a single stage actor playing multiple roles.

Scoops jumped to his feet, "well, I should get going too."

"Nice," Riley called back into the house, "what did you say, dad?"

Mr. Kushinski yelled back from inside the garage. "I told him about your obsession with stealing your little sister's bath bombs and toys."

"Nice dad!" Riley yelled back shaking his head.

"I don't have toys!" Charlotte's voice carried down the stairs.

As the boys walked back into the kitchen, Mrs. Kushinski was reading at the table.

"Thanks again for supper, Mrs. Kushinski."

"Yes, for sure any time Scoops," she replied as she got up to see him out.

As they stood at the door, Mr. Kushinski came back carrying a pair of gently used running shoes. They looked brand new to Scoops. "Big day tomorrow, son, you might need these."

They all looked down at Scoops shoes.

"Those certainly won't do," Riley chuckled.

"Wow, thanks, Mr. Kushinski," Scoops said with a smile. "Are you sure? Don't you need them?"

"My running days are over."

"Well, thanks, these are great." He looked at Riley as if waiting for his approval.

"Yeah for sure, try them on Scoops," Riley told him.

Scoops kicked off his old shoes, which flew off way too easily and put on the new runners. He hopped up and down, testing them out. "Wow, I'm going to leap like a deer in these," he said proudly. "Thanks, Mr. Kushinski!"

"No problem, next time we'll get you a haircut," he kidded.

"Why?" Scoops asked, brushing his hair out of his eyes.

Riley dropped a not so subtle hint that it was time for him to leave, "see you tomorrow Scoops."

Scoops caught his drift, "night, everyone, thank you again for everything." He turned and started to walk away.

"What a lovely young man," Mrs. Kushinski said as he made his way down the driveway.

Mr. Kushinski seconded with a smile.

Meanwhile, upstairs, Charlotte peered out from behind her curtains and watched as her prince walked away into the night.

11
TRUE COLOURS

Scoops walked down the sidewalk. His collar up, his hands in his pockets. Doing his best James Dean. He didn't exactly know where he was, so he headed back to his base camp, John Smith High School. From there, he could get home. As the school came into view, he saw a single car in the parking lot. He could just make out a couple of silhouettes in the field near the track. As he got closer, he recognized their voices. It was Randle and Todd. Uh oh, Scoops thought to himself. He stopped and looked around for an alternate route. The only way he knew would take him right passed them. What were they doing anyway, practicing discus? Hoping that they were distracted, he decided not to cut across the field and instead stick to the sidewalk.

"Atta boy, Todd," he heard Randle say.

"Atta boy, Todd," Scoops mimicked to himself, "way to hurl that discus. Nice job Todd, man you're so big and strong." He switched roles to play Todd, "Thanks, Randle pal, sure do appreciate that. I couldn't do it without you, little buddy."

100

Just before he could safely disappear into the residential area next to the field, he stopped in the dark to watch them. In the light of Randle's old Buick, he watched as Todd twirled and threw the discus. He can actually throw that thing a long way, Scoops thought. He watched for a couple of minutes then he moved on.

Scoops and his mom lived about eight blocks from the school, where the new houses turned into old apartments. They had rented out a suite on the ground floor, which made it a lot easier to haul boxes in from the patio rather than through a set of doors and up a flight of stairs. The apartment was a dump. There was no denying that, but it was home now. His mom and dad never did have much, and now, with his dad passing, it made things even worse. There was no insurance money because they never could afford the premiums, and there were no savings. Even the funeral had been a struggle. Thankfully, they had a few months to prepare for it. Even then, his dad didn't want one.

"Save the money," he had said from his deathbed. "You're going to need it." That was dad, always looking out for them, and he was right.

As Scoops stood on the street corner across from their apartment, waiting for the light to change, a car crawled up beside him.

"Well, well, well, look who it is," Randle said as he rolled down his window. "What is a nice girl like you doing out all alone on a night like this?"

Before Scoops could run, Todd had already opened his door and started walking around the front of the car. Scoops looked up and down the road. Although it wasn't even that late, they were the only people out. There was nowhere to hide, nowhere to run, and no help in sight.

He was going to have to face them alone. He closed his eyes tightly, pretending he was Clark Kent entering a phone booth. He opened them a brave new man.

"Well, good evening, Randle and Todd," Scoops greeted pleasantly. "You guys just get out of book club?"

By now, Randle had put the car in park and was getting out of the big boat too. "Hilarious," he said. "Where is your girlfriend?" he asked, alluding to Riley.

"I didn't think Todd wanted me to see his girl anymore?"

Todd grabbed him by the shirt. "Very funny," he said. "But you know what's funnier?"

"Not sure funnier is a word, but sure," Scoops entertained him, "what is funnier?"

"We're not on school property anymore. And there is no one around to protect you." Todd was holding Scoops' shirt tighter now, and it was starting to restrict blood flow to his head. Scoops' eyes began to burn, he gasped for air but didn't back down.

"Yeah, that is pretty hilarious."

Todd squeezed harder.

"Hey Randle, did you see those UFOs back by the school?"

"What are you talking about?" Randle snapped back.

"You didn't see them," Scoops choked. "Little discs flying in the air, you probably were looking too high, they were barely off the ground," he breathed heavily, "mowing the heads off the dandelions."

"Amusing," Todd tightened his grip. "Do I look like a guy that enjoys your sense of humour?"

Scoops toes were barely touching the ground. "Nope, you look like a guy who only knows one spelling for the word to."

Todd started to lift Scoops off his feet.

Scoops groaned. Things were going a little too far. "Sorry, Todd, I'm just kidding around."

Todd's eyes were cold and serious.

"Please," Scoops begged, gasping for breath, "please stop." He tried to hold himself up by grabbing Todd's forearms and shoulder.

As Scoops tried to cling to Todd, Randle saw the pair of shoes in his hands.

Todd was starting to enjoy watching Scoops in anguish too much. "What's the matter tough guy?" he asked viciously.

Randle snatched the shoes out of Scoops hands, ripping his skin as he did. "What's this Scoops?" he asked.

The lack of oxygen getting to Scoops brain was starting to make him woozy. He didn't bother to respond.

Randle looked at the old shoes in his hand and realized Scoops must be wearing something newer. He looked down at Scoops feet and saw the runners Mr. Kushinski had given him. "Did daddy buy you brand new runners for the big day?" He let out a menacing laugh.

Todd put his right foot behind Scoops and pushed him, tripping him into a large puddle. Scoops smashed his back hard on the ground, and his head snapped back, hitting an underground sprinkler head. Instantly, his clothes were soaked. The two figures above him started to become blurry, and he felt his shoes being ripped from his feet.

"Get them, Todd," he faintly heard Randle say. "Let's have a look."

As Scoops tried to yell at them to stop, Randle hurled his old shoes as hard as he could at his face. One missed, splashing in the water beside him, but the other struck him right in the lip. Instantly it burst open, and blood started to stream down his chin.

"Pass them here, Todd," Randle commanded.

Scoops sat up, holding the back of his head with his right hand and putting pressure on his lip with his left.

"Daddy couldn't even afford name brand shoes. What a pity," Randle jeered.

The boys laughed.

"Maybe Daddy just doesn't love you anymore."

"He doesn't," Scoops replied honestly. He rubbed his skull and felt his blood-soaked hair.

Both boys howled. "No kidding, how could he."

Todd grabbed the shoes from Randle and held them up in the moonlight. "These are garbage," he spit inside the shoes. "You think you are going to beat me in these?" he asked, laughing maniacally.

Randle leaned down beside Scoops, clenched his fist and swung it like a sledgehammer hard against his thigh, giving him a huge charley horse.

Scoops let out a shrill scream and grabbed at his leg. Without the applied pressure of his hand on his lip, his mouth began spurting out more blood.

"Just in case," Randle said. "Try jumping now."

Scoops fought back the tears as Todd took his new runners and held them under a puddle, filling them with muddy water.

Randle laughed. "Let's go, Todd. I think a car's coming."

"Peace," Todd said as he flexed his pecs.

Scoops didn't respond, he just laid back in the water and waited for them to leave. Although he was freezing the cold water felt nice against the back of his head. He would get his revenge tomorrow. He wasn't going to win this battle.

He listened to them get in the car and slam the doors. As they peeled off, he could hear them laughing through Randle's open window. As he sat in the puddle, soaked as a pond ornament he asked himself, is this even about the girls or do they really care that much about this discus hurling thing?

Scoops left both pairs of shoes outside to dry and made his way into the musty old apartment building. He immediately knew what every single one of his neighbours had for dinner. As he opened the door to the small apartment, he expected to have to explain his face, clothes, and the gash in the back of his head to his mother but fortunately, she wasn't home.

He peeled his soaked socks off, tossing them in a small pile and walked into the bathroom to check his wounds. As he admired his battle scars in the tiny mirror above the sink, he said to himself, "that's not so bad." He struck a fighting pose in the mirror and shouted at himself as if talking to Randle and Todd. "Is that all you got?" He bounced up and down until it reminded him how much his leg hurt. "I have taken number twos that have hurt more than this." He put his face up against the mirror to get a closer look at his lip. "That's not so bad. I don't think that will keep your girl from kissing me, Todd. Good try, though." He took a hot cloth and wiped the blood from his chin.

As he walked into the kitchen, he saw a note his mom had left him next to a small lamp.

Son,

I have to work tonight. Dr. Morgan's daughter is going to show me what I need to clean at the clinic. I shouldn't be late. I bought a loaf of bread, so have a slice of toast if you are hungry.

Love you, Mom
P.S Hope you had a great day and made nice friends.

"Nice friends for sure," Scoops said, reflecting on the Kushinskis. "And some real genuine stand-up guys named Randle and Todd," he added sarcastically.

He looked around the tiny apartment. It was almost 10:30 p.m. He walked to the couch and flopped down. Instantly he was reminded that his pants were soaking wet. He grabbed the remote and tried to turn on the television. There was no response. Another bill not paid. Scoops sighed and dropped the remote on the couch cushion next to him, and within seconds, was sound asleep.

12
TRACK DAY

Eager students packed the gym cramming in to listen to Mr. Pripps give an overview of the day's activities. They stood silently in orderly rows as if they were depicting the first Emperor of China's Terracotta Army. Along the walls, teachers and volunteer supervisors lined up like the Queen's Guard. As was typical at John Smith High School, there was hardly a whisper. Today was no different from any other, how dare there be any fun on track and field day.

Scoops' squeaking shoes announced their arrival when he and Riley entered.

Mr. Pripps immediately ran up to Riley. "How are you feeling this morning, Riley?"

The star athlete just nodded and raised a tall cup of coffee to his lips to take a sip.

"Coffee!" Mr. Pripps shrieked. "You can't drink coffee. It's race day!"

Principal Wentworth walked up to them in a panic. "Let's get going, Mr. Pripps," he barked. "Before the fire marshal comes." The Principal's anxiety wore off on Mr. Pripps, and he hurried to the podium to address the students.

"What happened to your lip, Scoops?" Riley asked.

"Nothing," he replied. His lip had swollen up considerably overnight. "Hey, there is Randle and Todd," he announced and started to march over to where they stood with Emily and Lisa. Back on school grounds, he was invincible again and back to his frivolous self. He was back in his comfort zone, and he was about to storm the beaches of Normandy (or for the sake of accuracy, Bormandy).

"Morning Randle and Todd," Scoops heckled, interrupting their conversation. "How are you two dial tones this fine morning?" he asked, giving them a thumbs-up.

The two boys turned, surprised to see him so calm and fearless after the beating they had laid on him the night before.

"Are you ready for the big day, Todd?" Scoops slapped him as hard as he could on the shoulder. "I see you have your shoes on the right feet, so that's a good start."

Todd stepped forward. "You want some more?" he grunted, puffing his chest.

"More what?" Lisa asked.

Randle intervened, "Nothing." He shot Todd a warning glance instructing him to be careful.

"What happened to your lip, Scoops?" Emily asked.

Scoops sluffed it off. "Nothing, I just bumped into Todd and Randle last night."

"What!" Lisa, Emily, and Riley said at once.

Todd and Randle looked petrified.

Scoops laughed. "Oh, it's not like that, they were very nice. They took me for ice cream."

Now everyone was surprised, including Randle and Todd. They exchanged looks as though they had made a fatal mistake in corroborating their story.

"It was great, really nice," Scoops continued, "until about five minutes after listening to them talk, I fell asleep out of sheer boredom and slammed my face against the table."

Thanks to having first-hand experience, the girls looked like they were buying the story.

"Why are your shoes wet?" Lisa asked.

"When I came to, Todd offered to show me how to throw a discus," he lied.

"Really?" Lisa asked frowning in disbelief.

Todd was too confused to say anything.

"Anyway," Scoops continued narrating his fable. "We were out in the field, just tossing the things." Scoops started acting it out, but it was obvious he had never even held a discus before. "Then the sprinklers came on." He tapped Todd on the chest as if they were best friends. "What a time, hey big guy?"

Todd nodded, not having a clue what was going on.

"Really?" Lisa asked doubtfully. She looked at Todd as if she was half-impressed.

"Nope!" Scoops came clean. "What kind of loser would go out in the dark and practice discus? I mean you would have to have nothing at all in your life. No cool friends, no personality, no girl to spoil..." Scoops kept muttering on.

Lisa turned to Todd, "I thought that is what you were going to do last night, Todd?"

Scoops, Riley, and Emily, began laughing.

Todd's face went from white to bright red.

Scoops tapped Todd on the shoulder and looked directly at Randle. "Don't be embarrassed Todd, at least you weren't the one who just went and watched."

Randle's face turned as red as Todd's.

"You know what you should practice next?" Scoops asked. He volunteered the answer before they could guess. "Holding your breath for longer than three minutes, now there is a feat we all could celebrate."

Riley and Scoops started laughing as the humiliated boys stormed off.

Mr. Pripps began to address the students. "Welcome to Track Day folks, we are going to get started right away. All the running events will be held this afternoon, so for those participating, please make sure you eat a hearty, healthy lunch, stay hydrated, stay loose..." he stared at Riley as if he was speaking directly to him.

Riley tapped Scoops on the shoulder, "Let's go Scoops. I'm hungry."

High Jump 9:30 a.m.

When Scoops and Riley showed up at 9:29, a small crowd had already formed by the high jump mat. Scoops had a small water bottle, and Riley was eating something wrapped in tinfoil.

When Mr. Pripps saw Riley he quickly ran over to him. "Riley, what are you eating?" he asked, his voice thick with worry.

Riley wiped his chin. "Breakfast burrito," he mumbled, not understanding why it would be of any concern.

"Riley, you can't eat that. It's going to give you cramps! You have to run today, remember?"

"This afternoon," Riley reminded him.

Mr. Pripps covered his face with his hands as if he couldn't bear to watch until a beeper went off in his pants. "Oh goodness, we have to get underway!" he shouted. "Scoops get over to the mat."

"Good luck, bud," Riley said. Then he walked to sit with Lisa and Emily, who watched from a small set of portable bleachers.

"No problem, I got this," Scoops replied confidently. "No worries, pal."

Randle saw Riley heading over to sit down and bounded over to make sure he beat him to sit next to Emily.

"Ok, let's get started," Mr. Pripps bellowed.

Scoops walked up to Todd, who was getting in the zone, stretching with his eyes closed.

"Scoops…!" Mr. Pripps cried.

Scoops stepped forward and immediately ripped off a pair of tear-aways as if called onto the court in the dying minutes of game seven.

"You will go last," Mr. Pripps finished.

Scoops threw his arms up and stared at the sky. "Ah, come on!" he protested. "I just took my pants off!"

"Todd!" Mr. Pripps shouted. "You're up first. We are going one person at a time, this isn't the Olympics."

Todd transitioned from his warm-up stretching to bouncing up and down.

Mr. Pripps called out the rules. "Each contestant will have three attempts at each level. Once you make it without the bar falling off, you can move to the next height."

"Got it, Coach!" Todd yelled at Mr. Pripps.

Mr. Pripps jumped and looked around startled, trying to locate whom Todd was addressing. "Everybody good?" he asked a final time.

"I'm good, Coach!" Todd yelled again.

This time, Mr. Pripps realized he was talking to him.

Scoops walked up to Todd to give him some last-minute advice, "over the bar Todd, like a deer, not under like an antelope."

Todd ignored him. He was in the zone.

"When you are ready, Todd," Mr. Pripps said.

Todd nodded his head and gave a thumbs-up signal as if he was a fighter pilot about to take off an aircraft carrier. Then he made a wide arch. He bounced on his tiptoes for the first few steps then started kicking his legs straight out in front of him like a Ukrainian dancer.

"Goodness," Scoops said as he watched him, "he is going to exhaust himself before he even gets there. What does he think he is doing, walking on the moon?"

When Todd got to the bar, he leaped and cleared it by a good six inches. His timing was spot on. When his back hit the landing mat, he rolled off and let out a big roar as if he had just dunked over three defenders.

Randle stood and cheered from the bleachers, "Yay Todd!" Then he realized he was the only one standing and sat down awkwardly.

Riley couldn't help it. "Yah! Good one, Todd—way to set the bar!"

The girls laughed, and Randle gave him a spiteful stare.

Todd bounced his way back to Scoops and hopped up and down beside him.

Scoops started bobbing his head in unison with Todd as if he was hopping too. "Good job, Todd," he congratulated, his head continuing to bob, "if they ever start doing this out of high school, you might have a future in it."

Todd began his wide arch. As he approached the raised bar, Scoops began to sportscast, "look at the grace, the sheer grit and determination."

Again, Todd cleared it and let out a huge roar.

Randle started to jump to his feet but caught himself.

"Yeah, you get 'em, tiger!" Scoops shouted at Todd. "Push it to the limit bud!"

Todd returned and stood by Scoops.

"You watching this?" He grunted at Scoops as he continued to hop up and down.

Scoops just stood staring at him, bobbing his head copying him, "can't take my eyes off it, Todd." The big guy looked at him, waiting for another insult or jab, but Scoops was waiting until he started his approach.

113

Todd began his wide arch.

"If only Lisa was here to see it," Scoops yelled at him.

Todd whipped his head to the bleachers to look for Lisa. It was too late. His timing was off, and as he jumped, his shoulder hit the bar knocking it off. As he hit the mat, he pointed at Scoops and shrilled, "do-over, a do-over, I want a do-over. He threw me off!"

"You can have two do-overs, Todd," Scoops reminded him. "How about that?"

Todd hopped back over to Scoops. "Don't throw me off again," he cautioned as he wiped the sweat from his upper lip with the back of his hand.

Scoops ignored Todd's warning as he watched him continue to hop up and down huffing and puffing. "What's the matter big bad wolf, the third little piggy's house giving you trouble? You know if your track and field career doesn't take off, you might want to try skipping. I think joining a good Jump Rope Team is a good fall back option for you."

Todd looked at Scoops sternly, "skipping is for losers." He started his second attempt.

"Well if that's the case they will probably let you be captain," Scoops hollered after him.

Todd looked back balefully at Scoops. His timing disrupted, he jumped straight up and came down right on the bar.

"Ah!" Todd growled. "He threw me off again." He ran over to Mr. Pripps. "Scoops is doing it on purpose, sir. Make him stop," he whined.

"Scoops," Mr. Pripps asked, much more politely than Todd was hoping. "Take a break, not this time alright. It is his last attempt."

Todd returned to his all too familiar starting hop. He shook his hands out beside him as he bounced up and down inhaling and exhaling slowly. Back in the zone, he began his approach. This time with his arms held straight out as if he was pretending to fly.

As he neared the bar fiercely flapping his wings, Riley shouted from the bleachers. "You can do it, Big Bird!"

Todd stutter-stepped and slipped as he tried to plant his foot. His legs flew out from under him, and he fell straight on his back, missing the mat completely.

The crowd groaned empathetically.

Todd rolled over quickly and started charging at Scoops.

"I didn't say anything!" Scoops defended himself, throwing up his hands in innocence. "I think you were just tired from all that hopping up and down. I thought you were going to pound yourself in the ground for a bit there. Maybe you should try to limbo under it," Scoops suggested.

Aware that Mr. Pripps was in the vicinity, Todd growled and walked back to the school.

"Todd, you got a little dirt there," Scoops said, pointing in a circular motion to his entire back.

Todd ignored him and continued walking across the field, dejected.

Lisa ran after him, but he just stretched his hand out as if to say no. Embarrassed, she stopped and returned angrily to her seat.

"Scoops, you're up!" Mr. Pripps shouted.

"Ready, Coach!" Scoops said, giving his best Todd impression. He grabbed his pants by the ankles and pulled hard, ripping apart every button except for the final one. "Ah, man!" he cried. "I wasted the good one."

"We're running out of time, Scoops. We will just leave the bar at the highest level. If you beat that you win, okay?"

Scoops gave a single, self-assured nod.

From behind him, Scoops heard a familiar voice. "Let's go Scoops. You got this!" It was Mr. Kushinski.

Scoops looked at him and gave him a casual thumbs-up. "No problem Mr. Kushinski, but you are going to want to watch closely, you won't be able to catch it on the highlight reel."

Scoops ran straight at the bar and tried to dive it as if he was a dolphin jumping through a hula-hoop. He caught it with his stomach, and it came crashing down beneath him.

The crowd went silent, staring as though they had just witnessed an innocent man publicly executed.

Scoops stood up and eyed the bar as two volunteers reset it. The crowd watched as he practiced some alternative options. No one said a word as he walked back to Mr. Pripps.

"Have you ever done this before?" Mr. Pripps asked.

"Yes, sir!" Scoops responded as if such an outrageous question surprised him. "I won last year at my school, just a little rusty that is all." He began to stretch.

"Alight," Mr. Pripps warned, "well, this is your second attempt."

"Thanks, sir. I will get it this time. I just need to find my form." This time, before diving, he sprinted at the mat as fast as he could. He caught his feet on the bar knocking it off again.

Laughter began to ripple through the crowd.

Scoops was undaunted, he rolled off the mat and started to examine the takeoff point. He pressed his toes on the grass.

"I think the ground is getting a bit soft," Scoops said as he jogged back to Mr. Pripps.

Mr. Pripps ignored him, "big day ahead Scoops, last attempt." The young gym teacher was already starting to pack up to move to the next event.

This time, Scoops took a different approach that began with a wide arch, similar to Todd (saving the hopping and seven-lords-a-leaping dance). As he got to the bar, he jumped and arched his back with impeccable timing. His feet followed as if his whole body was a huge wave cresting in the ocean. He cleared the bar with ease.

The crowd erupted with applause. Everyone stood and cheered. Everyone except Randle.

Discus: 11:00 a.m.

The toughest part of Scoops' entire high jump experience was buttoning back up his tear-aways that now seemed to have a million side snap buttons. As he stood, fussing with his pants, Riley, and his father approached him.

"Great job, bud," Riley said, offering Scoops a high five. "Didn't know you had it in you?"

Scoops replied honestly, "me neither."

"Come on," Riley argued, "you hustler you."

"Hustler, what do you mean?"

"You had that in the bag all the way. Way to show up the big idiot."

"I had no idea what I was doing, I totally lucked out," Scoops admitted.

"Really?" Mr. Kushinski asked. "At first, I was certain, but that last jump was perfect."

"Thanks," Scoops said gratefully. "All luck I assure you, I had no idea what I was doing."

"I don't believe it," Mr. Kushinski said as he watched Scoops continue to struggle button after button.

"You know you can just pull those things off like regular track pants, right?" Riley asked.

Scoops looked at him as if what he said was absurd. "No way, it just doesn't have the same effect." He finally finished doing his pants up and let out a heavy sigh. "It is all about intimidation buddy, wait until you see me toss this disc thing."

Mr. Kushinski started coaching as if he was an old pro. "Yeah, so make sure you keep your balance within the throwing circle and time the delivery perfect." He continued to babble on, but Scoops wasn't listening. He was looking around for the girls.

"Where are Lisa and Emily?" he asked Riley.

Mr. Pripps had just finished chalking the lines for the throwing sector as the boys neared the discus and shotput area of the field. Scoops walked down a boundary line as if he was a tightrope walker, slamming his foot down, making a cloud of dust with each step, his new shoes still wet and soaking up the dry chalk.

"Hey, get off the lines, Scoops!" Mr. Pripps bellowed still holding the chalk-marking machine in his hands. "I just marked those." He instantly noticed a bag of potato chips in Riley's hands as they walked up to the throwing circle. "Riley!" he yelled. "What are you eating now?"

"Just some chips," Riley said, straight-faced. "Chip?" he said, offering the bag to Mr. Pripps.

The teacher ignored the offer. "Did you forget you have to run today?"

"This afternoon," Riley corrected him again.

Mr. Pripps had been so focused on Riley he hadn't even noticed Riley's father. Mr. Kushinski stretched out his hand to introduce himself. "Good morning, I am Riley's dad, John."

Mr. Pripps shook his hand emphatically, his eyes wide with excitement. "Incredible," he said, looking Mr. Kushinski up and down as if he was a thoroughbred stallion and Riley was his pedigree. "Riley is the greatest runner I have ever seen. It's unbelievable." Mr. Pripps continued to give Mr. Kushinski the ESPN 30 for 30 on Riley's running career as the boys started their own conversation.

"Have you ever thrown a discus, Riley?" Scoops asked nervously.

"No man, you'll have to show me."

"Show you?" Scoops said eyes wide with fear. "I was relying on you to show me."

Riley stopped short and looked at Scoops dumfounded. "You have never done this before?"

"I have never done any of this before!" he shot back, "I told you that!"

"Oh boy," Riley said and slowly took a tiny bite of a chip.

"What do I do?" Scoops asked, his face turning pale.

"I don't know. You did well at high jump."

That wasn't good enough for Scoops. He scrunched up the chest of his bright yellow tank top in his hands. "Well, you have to know something. You're good at running."

"Running is different."

"Why?"

"Because with running," Riley paused thoughtfully, "I don't know, you just run."

Scoops nodded in agreement. "You're right. I should have done that."

"You tried to, remember?" Riley laughed. "You ran for like twenty feet."

"Oh yeah," Scoops replied as if he had already forgotten.

"Well good luck, I am going to go sit and watch with my dad."

Todd was back to doing a ridiculous amount of stretching. He snarled at Scoops as we walked up, then bent over to touch his toes. As his fingers dangled about six inches above his shoes, his tight black t-shirt rode up his back, exposing a mat of curly dark black hair. His shorts sagged, revealing the top of his butt crack.

"Hi Todd," Scoops said cheerfully as it was the first time he had seen him all day. He watched Todd grunting away, trying to reach his feet. With each attempt, his shirt rode up a little higher, and his shorts sagged just a bit lower. "Geez Todd, it is a good thing you can't touch your toes, or we would be in for quite a show."

Todd just looked at him with his head dangling upside down, his eyes bloodshot.

As Scoops mirrored Todd's stretches, Lisa and Emily walked out of the school and giggled as they approached them.

"What's so funny?" Todd barked.

"Nothing," Lisa replied, smiling at Scoops as they passed. The girls saw Riley and his dad sitting on the bleachers and went over to join them.

Enraged, Todd stopped stretching and stormed off to the discus circle, which was within about ten feet of the school. He walked up to one of the large glass windows that lined the library and stared at his reflection. One-way film covered each window, which allowed viewing from the inside out but not in. Todd checked his cheeks as if by some miracle, some of his back hair had spread to his face. Disappointed, he began consoling himself by turning from side to side, flexing his triceps.

Scoops watched, awestruck that he dared to do this in front of everyone outside, let alone whoever was inside, and there was.

Unbeknownst to anyone, Mr. Tillweed sat submissively on Miss Carpenter's desk as she gripped him by the lab coat.

"You've been checked out, and now you are overdue," she whispered to Mr. Tillweed seductively. "Now you are going to have to pay the fee."

As she moved in for a kiss, she saw Todd out of the corner of her eye. Her eyes widened, and she gasped in horror. Mr. Tillweed quickly spun around to look and saw Todd staring at the reflection of his buttocks.

Todd began clenching his butt cheeks.

Mr. Tillweed and Miss Carpenter stared back at him frozen as if he was a T-Rex that could only see them if they moved.

"He can't see us," Mr. Tillweed whispered.

"Are you sure," Miss Carpenter asked nervously.

"Yeah," Mr. Tillweed said as he slowly waved his hand back and forth.

By now, Todd had his hands down his shorts pulling out a wedgie.

Scoops walked up beside him, and instinctively they ducked again.

"I can't stand that kid!" Mr. Tillweed growled, his eyes bulging with hatred.

"Oh, Mr. Tillweed," Miss Carpenter said with a baby voice, "let me make you feel better." She pulled him by his coat and kissed him.

Back at the window, Scoops was back to copying every single movement Todd made.

"Todd you're up first again!" Mr. Pripps yelled. "Get over here."

Todd bolted to the discus circle, "I'm ready Coach!"

"Alright, here are the rules!" Mr. Pripps shouted. "Contestants each get three attempts. Remember, do not step out of the circle, and the discus has to land inside the lined area. Farthest throw wins. Got it?"

"Got it, Coach!" Todd yelled in his ear.

Scoops walked up to Todd, surprised to see him standing still. "I like your strategy, Todd," he crooned, "less bounce, that's a good idea, harness that energy."

"Spectators!" Mr. Pripps yelled. "Please pay attention. I don't want anyone getting hurt."

The contestants' eyes followed his voice to the bleachers.

Like a pimple on prom night, Dr. Fiore had appeared out of nowhere and sat amongst the small crowd next to Randle. Randle had slipped in and taken a seat next to Mr. Kushinski so he could keep an eye on Emily and Riley. Dr. Fiore looked intensely at Todd and gave him a thumbs-up.

Scoops saw the exchange and groaned.

Dr. Fiore's gesture stroked Todd's already inflated ego, and he laughed arrogantly. "Mr. Pripps, maybe you should warn them too." He pointed to some students about two hundred meters downfield. Dr. Fiore was the only one to think it was funny. He gave Todd another thumbs-up.

Riley caught sight of the exchange from three seats over and replicated the signal to Scoops. "Atta boy, Todd," Riley taunted, "dream big."

Todd stepped into the circle as if he was about to throw for the gold at the Olympics. He stared downfield, checked the positioning of his feet, then started his windup. He spun, his weight shifted, his technique was flawless. He released the discus, and it soared through the air.

"Wow great throw, Todd," Mr. Pripps said as he passed Todd the end of a tape measure and ran to the discus to measure the distance. "That has got to be a record."

"Have you been practicing, Todd?" Scoops wisecracked. "It is pretty light out here. Maybe you want to close your eyes."

"Holy, fifty-two meters, that's incredible." Mr. Pripps said excitedly.

"What does it say on your end, Todd?" Scoops asked.

Todd looked down into his hands, "zero."

Everybody on the bleachers laughed.

Todd gritted his teeth snarling at Scoops.

"Alright big guy, try again. This time try to plant your foot a little bit earlier, really get that torque," Mr. Pripps coached.

Scoops rolled his eyes at Riley and Mr. Kushinski.

Riley responded by cupping his hand behind his ear and pointing at Mr. Pripps and Todd. "Get some tips," he mouthed.

Scoops just shrugged him off. Instead, he looked at Lisa and gave her a quick wink.

She reciprocated, almost stopping his heart in an instant.

Thud!

"Great throw," Mr. Pripps urged Todd on and again ran out into the field with the tape. "Fifty-four meters, I can't believe it."

Todd double fist pumped and grunted.

Scoops was still in heaven and decided to let Todd off the hook. He stared back at Lisa, and she gave him another big smile. Dr. Fiore and Randle were too enthralled with Todd's record-shattering performance to notice. He had her full attention, and that was all he needed. "I think she is falling for me," Scoops whispered to himself. "You are in trouble now, girl," he mumbled, suddenly filled with the confidence of a real womanizer.

Emily caught Lisa and him looking at each other and nudged Riley with her left shoulder. As if they were passing a note through class, Riley poked Mr. Kushinski, who in turn tapped Randle having no idea who he was.

Randle's beady eyes widened as he saw Lisa and Scoops flirting. "Lisa, you should come and sit by your dad!" he said, standing up and inviting her to take his seat. It was the perfect solution because it would allow him to slide in next to Emily.

Emily shot him a venomous look.

Thud!

"Wow, Todd! Great throw again," Mr. Pripps praised.

The song was on repeat and Scoops was getting bored and slightly annoyed.

"Way to beat your last throw. Fifty-five meters," Mr. Pripps said as he skipped back toward the throwing circle.

"You might as well just stay out there, Mr. P!" Scoops yelled as he confidently walked into the circle next to Todd.

"Yeah right, try beating that," Todd boasted to Scoops.

"No problem," Scoops said confidently.

Scoops stepped forward, rolling a discus down the field like a bowling ball.

It whipped through Mr. Pripps legs. "What the—"

"Hey," Todd cried as if he had never thought about rolling it and overlooked the technique.

"Nice try Scoops," Mr. Pripps said, trying to catch his breath. "Doesn't count, has to be in the air."

"No problem," Scoops replied. He picked up another discus and looked at Mr. Pripps. "Just take this, and throw it down there?" he said, pointing downfield.

"Yep, and you have to keep it between the lines," Mr. Pripps responded while winding back up the fifty-five feet of tape from Todd's third throw.

"I got it, Coach." Scoops stuck his tongue out as he started his windup. He spun hard, planted and threw the discus straight down into the grass about six feet in front of him.

Thwap!

It stuck into the ground like a crashed flying saucer.

A murmur rippled through the crowd.

"How far is that?" he asked as if it was going to be close.

Mr. Pripps just ignored him and kept winding the tape in.

The field was silent except for the tape measure retracting. Scoops grew impatient and started to pace off the distance from the circle to the discus. It was a generous two paces.

"Three meters!" Scoops yelled to the crowd.

The crowd erupted in applause.

Mr. Pripps couldn't help but smile.

Todd once again began his lonely walk of shame back to the school. This time, Lisa remained sitting and let her dad, Dr. Fiore run to catch up with him.

"One more attempt Scoops," Mr. Pripps told Scoops. "You have another miracle in you?"

"Yep," Scoops replied positively.

Just as he was about to throw his third and final attempt, there was a honk from the parking lot. Principal Wentworth hung out of his window, waving to all the students. "Good luck, everyone, and have fun!" he yelled as he nearly steered into a curb. He gave a final wave and drove off. His small Prius jerking and sputtering as he attempted to shift gears and roll the window back up at the same time.

"Bet he regrets not getting the elite package," Scoops said sarcastically, "at least he got the full size."

Mr. Pripps smiled and almost laughed but contained himself.

Scoops was curious. "Where's he going, anyway?"

"He has that concert downtown tomorrow he has to rehearse for, remember?" Mr. Pripps replied.

"Oh yeah, the symphony or something, right?"

Mr. Pripps had already moved on and was fully committed to making sure Scoops nailed his next attempt. "Alright Scoops, here you go, you got this." He patted him on the back and gave him a warm, encouraging smile.

Before starting his last windup, Scoops looked around the field. Teachers and volunteers patrolled the grounds as if it was a prison yard. Scoops thought about what Riley had said about the teachers, and how they didn't care. He looked at Mr. Pripps as he nodded in anticipation for Scoops to throw and thought to himself. There is one exception. This guy isn't that bad.

Scoops shook his head to refocus and restarted his windup. This time, Scoops had the momentum, he had the torque, and he had the balance. What he didn't have was the timing. He released the discus about 20 degrees too late.

The entire crowd went silent as the discus arched through the air towards the school crashing through one of the large library windows. A horrific scream coming from inside the library muffled the sound of shattering glass. Then there was a moment of deathly silence as everyone stared wide-eyed at Mr. Tillweed and Miss Carpenter locked in a heated embrace.

Scoops broke the silence. "It looks like Mr. Tillweed is enjoying another popsicle."

Mr. Pripps face went from a look of complete shock to total enlightenment.

"Guess we should be moving on," Scoops said nonchalantly. He folded his arms behind him and strolled off peacefully as if he was walking through a botanical garden.

200 Meter Sprint: 1:00 p.m.

Following a big hearty lunch in the school cafeteria, Riley and Scoops made their way back out to the track. The sun was shining brightly in the clear blue sky, and a nap seemed like a much better idea than running on a hot rubber track.

As if on cue, Mr. Pripps ran up beside them as they walked across the field. "How you feeling, Riley?" he asked, rubbing his belly. "My stomach is full of butterflies, you?"

"Feeling great thanks," Riley replied, "nice and full too."

"What did you eat?"

Riley looked at him as if the teacher was losing his mind, "just some chili and fries, sir."

"Chili and fries!" Mr. Pripps choked.

"And a large coke," Scoops added.

"Yeah," Riley remembered, "and a large coke, sir."

"A large coke?" Mr. Pripps gasped. "You need to be hydrating Riley. Coke is a diuretic."

"Diarrhea?" Scoops asked squinting.

"Diuretic," Mr. Pripps repeated.

"Yeah, that is what I said I think," Scoops said nodding. "You might need some Preparation H buddy."

"What's that?" Riley asked.

"I think it is for your…" he paused, "your you know what?"

"My what?"

"Butt."

"Diuretic," Mr. Pripps repeated for the third time, "not diarrhea. Preparation H is for hemorrhoids."

"Are you sure?" Scoops asked.

"Yes," Mr. Pripps nodded.

"Well, what does Preparation A thru G do?" Scoops asked quizzically. "Maybe one of those will help."

"Never mind," Mr. Pripps said, shaking his head.

"Hey, where did your dad go?" Scoops asked Riley looking around the field to spot him.

"He had to run back to the office for a bit, but he said to tell you he will try to make it back for your run."

"Really?" Scoops asked, enjoying the attention.

"Yeah," Riley replied, "he seems to be really interested in watching you. Not sure why."

Scoops hit him on the shoulder, "well, didn't you see me at high jump and discus? I'm awesome!"

The boys chuckled.

When they got to the track, Todd was leading Randle through some stretches.

"What, you are running now? What are you some kind of machine?" Todd snickered at Scoops.

Randle jumped in, "yeah, a real Jill of all trades," he snorted, "master of none."

Nobody laughed.

As they stood awkwardly watching Randle struggle to stretch out his legs, Riley whispered to Scoops. "He looks like a fawn trying to stand up for the first time."

As they laughed, Emily ran up behind them.

"Hey guys, you going to watch Lisa? She runs at 1:00 p.m. too."

"Randle has a race." Todd glared at her disgusted she would even think of it.

Randle pointed at Scoops, "Yeah, this clown is going down again." He stood on one foot to stretch out his thigh. He let out a wicked laugh and tried to grasp the foot of his other leg behind him. He couldn't keep his balance and began hopping in a circle trying to grab his shoe.

"Need a little help there, Randle?" Riley snickered. "You look like a one-legged pirate missing a peg leg."

"Todd," Scoops said concerned. "I think his butt might be on fire."

"No," Randle snarled, giving up and instead tried to touch his toes. He bobbed up and down, hardly reaching his knees with his fingers.

"Are you sure?" Riley asked again, "you look a little stuck."

"Try pulling your shorts down a bit," Scoops suggested, "that seems to help Todd."

The boys laughed and decided to give it a rest. Todd and Randle were doing enough to embarrass themselves in front of Emily.

"Todd, you should go watch Lisa," Emily hinted. "No one is watching her."

"What about her dad?" Scoops asked.

Emily shook her head no, "he got a call and had to leave."

"He should have seen that coming, being a psychic and all."

"Psychiatrist," Todd corrected Scoops.

"Yeah." Scoops turned and looked at Emily. "Wait, so he missed her win high jump and discus, made it in time to watch Todd, and now left again missing her last event?"

"Yep," Emily replied, still sending daggers at Todd with her eyes.

"Are you running anything today, Emily?" Scoops asked her.

"No, not today," she said. "Glad too, I'm wiped. I had to work late last night."

"Oh yeah, what do you do?"

"I just help my parents," she answered. "Good luck Scoops," she said and ran off to where Lisa was lining up.

Mr. Pripps shouted, "everybody line up!"

Scoops, Randle, along with five other boys, made their way to the starting blocks.

"Good luck, Scoops!" Mr. Kushinski shouted.

Scoops heard him and turned around quickly. He had a big smile. "Thanks, sir, glad you made it back."

"Nice shoes," Mr. Kushinski yelled and winked at Scoops.

"On your mark!" Mr. Pripps hollered from the starting line.

"You are going down, Scoops," Randle jeered.

Scoops just stood upright, watching Lisa on the other side of the track.

"Get set!" Mr. Pripps boomed.

By now, Randle was in a fully crouched position.

"Get 'em, Randle!" Todd yelled.

Scoops put his arms in a running stance but didn't bend his knees.

BOOM!

The starting gun went off, and the boys exploded out of the blocks. Scoops just stood watching Lisa warming up across the track.

"Go!" Mr. Pripps yelled at Scoops frantically, trying to re-fire the handgun. "Go! Go! Go!"

"It's ok Mr. P," Scoops said calmly, waving for him to stop. He turned and started to jog across the field to the other side of the track where Lisa was just lining up.

"Go Lisa!" he yelled as loud as he could.

Emily and Riley ran to catch up to him.

She turned and smiled when she saw the three of them running across the field to watch her.

By the time Randle wheezed his way across the finish line, all the other runners, and his loyal buddy Todd were already waiting for him. As he put his hands on his knees and panted like a wounded water buffalo, he and Todd looked across the track to see Emily, Riley, and Scoops cheering for Lisa as she broke through the finish-line ribbon.

3,000 Meter: 2:00 p.m.

"Riley," Mr. Pripps asked intensely. "How are you feeling?"

Riley looked at him as he cracked open a Pepsi. "Feeling pretty good, thanks."

Mr. Pripps immediately swatted the pop can out of his hands. It smashed hard against the grass, splashing everyone around them. He grabbed Riley by both shoulders. "Focus kid, this is it, you need to focus."

Mr. Kushinski watched the gym teacher's plight from the bleachers with both sympathetic eyes and a smile. Mr. Pripps turned to him and started evangelizing.

"You have to see your boy. I have never seen anything like it. He is going places, sir. I have no doubt about it." He focused his attention back on attempting to motivate and inspire Riley. "The 3,000 is your event, Riley."

"Are we doing this thing or what?" Randle called to them from the starting blocks as if he had just set the world record for the 200-meter dash.

"We're coming," Mr. Pripps snapped back. "Don't worry about these kids, Riley. Don't even pay attention to them. I want you to focus on getting the record. I know you can do it. Think big son. Think scholarship big."

Mr. Kushinski's ears perked up, dollar signs danced in front of his eyes, "go get 'em, son!"

Riley made his way to the starting blocks.

"About time, Riley," Randle said, "man you're slow."

Riley didn't respond.

"On your mark, get set," Mr. Pripps hollered with the red starting gun pointing up into the clear blue sky above them.

BOOM!

The boys were off.

"Come on, Riley, come on, Riley!" Mr. Pripps yelled oblivious to the scowls on the faces of the other racers' parents that lined the bleachers.

Within seconds, Riley had left a huge gap between him and the nearest racer. He bounded effortlessly around the track.

Mr. Pripps yelled at Mr. Kushinski as he ran back over. "See I told you, sir, look at him go!" He looked to the heavens as if he was going to sing a song of praise but then quickly cast his eyes back on Riley. "Look at him go!" he repeated. "He is almost done a lap already." He clapped and started hopping up and down in excitement. "He makes those other kids look like they are running the other way."

Ten angry sets of eyes stared him down.

"Hey," a proud mother shouted. "You are supposed to be impartial, what kind of coach are you?"

Mr. Pripps scoffed at her. "Come on, are you watching the same race?"

Mr. Kushinski's face started to turn red as he became more embarrassed and felt more uncomfortable.

"It is just a race," the angry mother protested.

"Just a race," Mr. Pripps barked. "You should tell your kid that. He looks like he thinks it's a walkathon." He waved his hand in disgust and jogged back to run alongside the track with Riley as he passed. "Go, Riley, go!"

Although Mr. Pripps was having the time of his life, Scoops was incredibly bored.

"What are you girls doing tonight?" he asked Emily and Lisa.

Todd leaned forward slowly. Somehow, he had managed to weasel his way in and sit down next to Lisa. He answered for them. "Nothing."

Scoops jumped back on guard. "I wasn't talking to you, Todd!"

Todd growled and put his arm around Lisa.

It didn't deter Scoops. "You girls want to hang out or something?"

Todd leaned forward again. "Nope, they already have plans with us."

"What plans?" Scoops asked, growing increasingly annoyed with Todd's presence. "It looks like your little buddy Randle won't be able to walk for the rest of his life." He pointed at Randle, who was last again. Severely struggling as he approached them. "He looks like a five-hundred-pound man chasing an ice cream truck."

Riley had lapped him at least twice already.

"He will be fine," Todd fired back.

"When?" Scoops jeered. "After you run him a bath full of Epsom salts?"

The girls laughed.

Mr. Pripps was on the other side of the track running alongside Riley cheering and rooting for him. He looked like a horse trainer working a horse in a round corral.

"Randle will be fine," Todd repeated, trying to convince himself.

"Are you sure? He looks like a salmon trying to swim upstream." Scoops prodded. "You should tell him just to spawn and die already."

"Shut your mouth!" Todd roared. "I'm warning you."

Scoops continued to egg him on. "Honestly Todd, I think Riley has passed Randle more times than Randle has passed us."

Todd bolted up. "That's it!" he yelled. "Do you want another beating? How is your lip, smarty-pants? Want me to hit you in the face with those ugly shoes too?"

"What?" Lisa gasped.

Mr. Kushinski heard him and was about to step in, but Lisa had it under control. She looked a lot more intimidating than he ever could.

"You did what?" she snarled. "You said you never touched him."

135

Todd started to stutter, "Well, maybe a little."

"That's it," she said and stood up fuming. "Come on, Emily. We are going out with Riley and Scoops tonight."

Scoops was even more surprised than Todd was. "Nice," he cheered, eyes wide but still able to squeeze out a quick wink at Todd. "You won't mind will you Todd?" Scoops jumped off the edge of the bleachers. "I better go and tell Riley."

When Scoops made his way up to the track, Mr. Pripps was still hollering at Riley. "One more lap buddy, one more lap." He looked down at the stopwatch in his palm. "You're going to beat the National record by a landslide, Riley!"

"Riley!" Scoops called. "Riley, guess what?"

"What?" Riley asked. Not a sliver off exhaustion in his voice as he passed.

"Lisa and Emily want to go out with us tonight."

Riley stopped on a dime. "Really?" he asked as he started to walk towards Scoops. There was not a bead of sweat on his body.

"What are you doing, Riley?" Mr. Pripps cried out. "What on earth are you doing?"

Riley ignored him.

"Where do they want to go?" he asked Scoops as he looked at the girls waiting by the bleachers.

"I don't know?" Scoops replied.

"What are you doing, Riley?" Mr. Pripps cried out again, grabbing Riley by the shoulders.

"Didn't you hear, sir? The girls want to go out."

"Yeah but you're almost done," Mr. Pripps said, tears filling his eyes.

"Just finish." He looked down at the stop clock and held it up to Riley's face. "Look you can still beat the record. You only have one lap to go!"

"Sorry sir, I have to go, I will finish on Monday."

Mr. Pripps fell to his knees, reaching for Riley's legs as if to try to drag him back to the track. Then he dropped to his stomach and started ripping clumps of grass out of the field.

"He is going places, no doubt about it," Mr. Kushinski said as he walked up to the sprawling gym teacher.

The two men watched the four teenagers as they walked across the field back to the school.

13
THE BIG DATE

"It is too bad my car is in the shop," Scoops said as he and Riley met up with Emily and Lisa in the school parking lot. "I picked a bad day to get her in for a tune-up."

Emily and Lisa already knew better than to entertain him.

Scoops had changed back into the same old worn out blue jeans and sweater that he had worn on his first day of school. Even after a day full of activity, his shoes still made a squishing sound as he walked across the hot pavement.

Riley had changed into a plain white polo and a pair of camo cargo shorts. "What do you girls feel like doing?" he asked, sticking to the basics. "Are you hungry?"

Both girls were too careful to admit it.

"I could eat," Scoops volunteered.

"I guess so," Emily chimed in. "Are you hungry, Riley?" she asked. Emily had quickly changed into a pair of blue jeans and a yellow hoodie. A black headband held her blonde hair out of her eyes.

Scoops answered for him, "Riley is always hungry, aren't you, buddy?" Scoops slapped him on the back.

Riley's mind was racing as they walked along. Where should they go? What should they do? He wasn't ready for this, and he couldn't blow this once in a lifetime opportunity.

"Riley?" Scoops nudged him. "What do you think?"

"Well, we could go to Antonio's?" he suggested. Antonio's was a decent Italian restaurant in the area and the only idea he had.

Emily scoffed, "okay Randle, can I order for myself this time?"

Riley's face reddened with embarrassment as he realized he had just made the most cliché suggestion possible. Besides, they would never get in the way they were dressed.

"Or we could go to Bridgeport Fun Park?" he offered.

"Bridgeport, what, who?" Scoops asked.

"Yeah what?" Lisa added. "Are we celebrating someone's tenth birthday or something?" Lisa wore a pair of floral print skinny pants with a baggy long-sleeved white knitted sweater. Her hair was tied back in a simple ponytail.

Scoops chuckled at her joke as if he knew what she meant, "yeah Riley, is it your birthday or something?"

"I think that is a very good idea," Emily said. "I have always wanted to go there."

"Really?" Lisa frowned.

"Come on, it will be fun," Emily nudged her. "We're not dressed up anyway, and you always say you want to try something different."

"From Randle and Todd?" Riley laughed. "Oh yeah, it'll be different."

The girls giggled in agreement.

Scoops was lost. "Alright, what is this Fun Park?"

Riley smiled as he explained, "this place with mini-golf, arcade games, batting cages and stuff like that."

Scoops eyes widened with excitement, "go-karts?"

"Yeah, I think so," Riley responded, "and food."

Scoops ran ahead a few steps and jumped in the air clicking his heels. "This is gonna be epic!" he hollered. "Nice one, Riley!"

Bridgeport Fun Park was certainly more than just a few blocks away. When the four teens finally arrived, the consensus was to eat first, so they made their way to the small restaurant that bordered the games area.

Scoops was exhausted. "Hopefully, there is a table," he said as herds of small children pushed passed them. It was Friday, no doubt their busiest time of the week.

As they waited at the hostess stand, a large waitress pulling double duty came up to greet them. She was about sixty years old and looked as though she either was about to retire or expire in the next ten minutes.

"For how many?" she asked with an ashy voice.

Riley answered, "Four, please."

"Non-smoking," Scoops added.

The tired lady looked Scoops up and down then started to cough into her elbow. "We don't have smoking and non-smoking sections," she rasped. "Haven't for over ten years. If you want to smoke, you are going to have to do it outside in the designated areas."

"That won't be necessary, ma'am," Riley stated.

"Just someplace quiet," Scoops added.

The big waitress turned and looked behind her at the crowded restaurant crammed full of screaming kids. She turned her head back around to Scoops, and her eyebrows rose as if a pair of gears connected the two. She reached into her apron and pulled out a pack of cigarettes and a lighter. "You on a date or something?" She tapped the lighter against the pack of cigarettes, "how romantic."

Riley motioned to the pack of cigarettes in the lady's nicotine-stained hands, "just so that you know, you can't smoke those in here."

Her mouth dropped open, revealing her discolored and decaying teeth. Between the chipped, broken and missing teeth, it was clear she wasn't working with a full set. "That's funny," she said as she rubbed her forearm against her brow. She stopped and looked at the girls. "How's the date going?" she started chuckling, which quickly transitioned into a dry coughing fit.

Riley looked over at Scoops, then over at the two girls who were staring at the floor uncomfortably.

"It's great," Riley nodded and studied her nametag. Then he gently tapped on the hostess stand, "it's going great, thanks, Rhonda."

"Looks like it," Rhonda replied. She rolled her eyes. "Follow me." She sighed heavily immediately leading to shortness of breath and wheezing for air.

A few hacks later and a couple of dusty nose blows the grotesque women finally sat the group down at a booth for four. Emily sat down first, and Lisa immediately sat down right beside her, forcing Riley and Scoops to squeeze in next to each other.

"What do you feel like having?" Riley asked awkwardly. He realized he needed to up his game and wasn't sure how he was going to accomplish it.

Lisa opened her menu, and an avalanche of crumbs fell into her lap. Disgusted, she brushed the debris off her pants onto the dirty floor.

"Not too sure, what do you guys feel like?" Emily asked, putting forth her best effort to appear optimistic.

"Nothing greasy," Lisa said snobbishly.

"Great thinking," Scoops said, "we don't want any grease on our hands while we're putting."

"No, I mean—" she cut herself off, "never mind." She was already starting to regret the decision to go out, let alone to Bridgeport Fun Park.

"What are we playing anyway?" Riley asked.

Lisa responded optimistically as if answering nothing might still be on the table, "what do you mean?"

Riley explained, "Like do you want to play teams, every man for themselves?"

Scoops jumped in to cast his lots, "teams, I want to be on Lisa's team." He went to high five her. "We are the only ones who won any events today, hey buddy?"

Lisa left him hanging.

"How about we play girls versus boys?" Emily suggested as she kicked Lisa under the table. Lisa had pulled her phone from her pocket and was about to check her messages.

"I like that idea," Riley said.

Scoops shook his head from side to side as if it was the worst idea ever.

Lisa was preoccupied, looking at her phone.

"And we should put a wager on it," Emily proposed.

"I like that even more," Riley said smiling. "And what will that be?"

"I say dinner?" Scoops contributed, and then suddenly went silent when he realized he didn't have any money and was already relying on Riley to pay.

"No," Riley quickly responded going all in, "how about a kiss?"

Emily laughed, "how about another date?"

It was a good compromise.

"Deal!" Riley agreed. Hope began to seep from his pores.

As Emily and Riley continued to flirt back and forth, Scoops watched Lisa, who nervously thumbed her phone.

After a minute, Lisa looked up pale-faced and softly whispered to Emily, "my dad just messaged me, asking where I am."

Emily's smile vanished. "What did you write back?"

"Nothing?" Lisa said as she tossed her phone on the table.

"Emilio?" Scoops asked. He started rubbing his chin as if he was brushing a goatee. "Not sure he is a real big fan of ours."

Riley laughed and corrected him, "you mean Dr. Fiore."

"Yes, pardon me," Scoops responded as if he had just sworn in a live broadcast. "Dr. Fiore."

Emily hid a big smile from Lisa with her hand.

"What does he want?" Riley asked. "Is he asking how you did today, seeing how he missed it all?"

Scoops scoffed. "Yeah, he probably wants to make sure you know how well Todd did."

"What did he want?" Emily repeated Riley's question.

"To know where we are?" Lisa mumbled softly.

Scoops banged the table with his fists and threw his palms up into the air. "I thought he was a psychic, doesn't he already know where we are!"

"Psychiatrist!" the rest of the table corrected him.

"Well he isn't very good at it, is he?" Scoops blurted back.

The tired waitress had made her way back to the table. The smell of tobacco ringed off her. "Are you ready to order?" she asked between wheezes.

"I should go," Lisa said, looking at Emily. "My dad is going to kill me."

Instantly Scoops' eyes widened in fear.

The four began talking as if Rhonda wasn't even there.

"No, you can't go," Riley complained.

"Yeah, I don't want to go," Emily said, causing a smile to explode on Riley's face and his heart to beat faster.

"Todd is going to tell him where we are."

"Well, how does Todd know where we are?" Riley asked Lisa.

Scoops chimed in, "yeah, he is probably still back at school waiting for Randle to finish running." He laughed and went to high five Riley.

Riley didn't see him because he was staring at Lisa.

Rhonda tapped her pen impatiently against an old notepad, "want me to come back in a few minutes?"

"No!" Scoops quickly shouted as if Rhonda didn't have another minute left to live. "We'll have four Cokes and a large meat lover's pizza please."

Lisa shot him a look.

"Hawaiian then?" Scoops said, raising his shoulders.

Before Lisa could stop her, Rhonda had faded out of the room like an ember in an ashtray. All that remained was the tobacco aroma that chased after her.

"You don't like meat lovers?" Scoops asked Lisa.

"Scoops," Lisa vented. "It's not the pizza. It's not you. It's just that my dad is…" she searched for words.

"A bit of a jerk," Scoops filled in the blank.

"Well no," Lisa tried to find a softer way to put it.

"A wet toilet seat?"

"No."

"A damp towel?"

"No."

"An empty roll of toilet paper?"

Lisa put her hand on her head. "Are you just describing things you don't like when you're in your bathroom?"

"No," Scoops denied and moved to another room.

"An itchy rug?"

"No!" Lisa said, raising her voice. "He is just very particular when it comes to who I date."

"He is?" Scoops asked furrowing his brow. "But he lets you date Todd?" He put his elbows on the table and leaned forward. Things were getting serious. "That guy is a total deadbeat, a major snooze fest. How could your dad like him?"

"Well," Lisa stammered, trying to defend him. "He is athletic, smart, and…" she hesitated, "well off."

"Oh," Scoops said, slapping his palms on the table, "he can throw a plate. Big deal." He glossed over the intelligence debate. "Well off," he scoffed, "more like well on…" he pointed at Lisa, "well on his way to the Town of Boredom population you and him."

"He is not that bad," Lisa argued.

Emily and Riley sat back in the booth uncomfortably while the two bickered back and forth.

"Come on," Scoops said, flailing his hands in the air, "if he were a two-sided coin with dull and fun on it, he would land on dull every time."

Lisa became even more defensive, "a two-sided coin, as opposed to a three-sided coin?"

Emily sensed the tension rising to another level and decided to diffuse the situation. "Girls versus boys, right?"

"Yep," Riley responded. "Start with mini-golf, then go-carts and then we need to decide on a finale in case we need a tiebreaker." He eyed Emily down, "which we probably won't."

Lisa and Scoops just sat, continuing to glare at each other.

"What's the finale?" Lisa asked sourly, ready to take Scoops down at anything.

"Final event," Scoops mumbled under his breath, "it's Italian. I thought you would know that. Dr. Fiore would."

Riley quickly continued before the two went at it again. "The arcade, ten dollars or fifteen minutes whatever comes first. The team who wins the most tickets wins."

Emily gave a single confident nod, indicating she accepted the terms. "You guys are going down," she promised.

"Yeah," Lisa grumbled, looking directly at Scoops. "Our food better get here quickly so we can get on with beating you and get out of here."

"Why, are you helping Todd with his arithmetic tonight?" Scoops asked. "Does he need someone to hold the flashcards? Maybe he needs help putting his supplements in alphabetical order or sorting his stamp collection by country of origin?"

Lisa ignored him and looked around for Rhonda. "She hasn't even brought us our drinks yet."

"Relax, Lisa, stop being so uptight," Emily said. "It is going to be fine."

Lisa found no comfort in Emily's words. "Where is she?" Lisa asked impatiently.

"She is probably back outside in the smoking section." Scoops answered.

Lisa cracked a smile.

Mini-Golf: 5:15 p.m.

When Scoops caught up to Lisa, she was already halfway to the mini-golf course.

Emily and Riley trailed behind lost in each other's eyes.

"I am sorry," he said as he caught up to her. "I didn't mean to upset you. I guess—"

Lisa cut him off, "I know, it is just that my dad isn't the easiest guy to get along with okay?"

Scoops bit his tongue.

"I am having fun, but in the back of my mind, all I can think about is what is going to happen when I get home."

For once, Scoops did not have much to say. "I'm sorry for that too," he said softly.

Lisa thanked him with a warm smile.

"I love your smile," he offered sweetly.

She giggled and took out her ponytail, letting her long dark hair blanket her shoulders.

Emily and Riley had caught up to them.

"Let me pay for golf," Riley offered.

"No, I can," Scoops protested, pretending to fumble through his jeans, looking for his wallet. Everybody knew he didn't have one.

"No, I can get it thanks though, Scoops," Riley said, patting him on the shoulder, "you can get the tokens."

"Tokens?" Scoops echoed anxiously. His lips moved confessing to everyone that he was slowly doing the math, ten multiplied by four - forty bucks!

The lady at the mini-golf desk was slightly friendlier than Rhonda, the waitress. She looked as though she also frequented the smoking section and even less frequently visited herself in a mirror. She plopped four coloured golf balls and a scorecard on the desk and painfully squeezed out, "have fun."

"Do you have a pencil?" Emily asked, pleasantly.

Slightly happier Rhonda let out a huge sigh as if to let them all know, this once, and only this once she would look under the desk and see if any pencils had somehow mysteriously found their way back into the typically empty container labeled 'pencils'.

Tapping his finger on the scorecard, Riley gently explained, "We need a pencil to keep score."

As she fingered under the desk for a pencil, she looked blankly at Riley.

Scoops stepped forward to elaborate. "You see, the scorecard is only really helpful if you can record the score on it," he paused, letting it sink in, "with a pencil."

Miraculously she found one and slammed it loudly on the desk. She let out another exasperated sigh. "I know what the pencil is for."

"Thanks," Emily said sweetly, batting her eyelashes.

Riley snatched the pencil out of her hand and held it up within two inches of the lady's face. "Now, might you have a sharpener under there?" he said, shaking the pencil drawing her attention to the fact it had no tip.

"Nope," she said.

"Another pencil?" Emily suggested.

"Never mind," Lisa said. She grabbed the pencil and whittling back the wood from the lead with her thumbnail. "This will work."

"How resourceful," cheerful Rhonda said, rolling her eyes.

"Speaking of resourceful," Scoops snarled. "You look awfully drained, why don't you take five? Don't let this strenuous job stress you out or break your spirit."

Lisa and Emily looked at Scoops bracing themselves and prepared to run.

Scoops continued to erupt, "Maybe if you didn't have to walk to the designated smoking section every fifteen minutes, you would have a bit more energy to locate and sharpen some pencils!"

Numbly the lady inched her way off her stool and left the booth as if Scoops' rant had somehow reminded her she needed a nicotine fix.

Scoops called after her, "There you go, and doesn't that exercise already give you a shot of energy. You keep it up, and your fibromyalgia and varicose veins will disappear in a week!"

She ignored him as she limped her way to the smoking area.

Scoops turned around to see his three friends staring at him with their eyes wide open. He blew out a big breath of air as if he acknowledged he had overreacted just a tad, "well, shall we?"

They nodded.

"Do you think she will say hi to Rhonda for us?" Scoops asked.

By the fourth hole, the girls had a six-shot lead, and Scoops was on the seventh hole trying to figure out how to skip his ball off the rocks, over the water, bounce if off the path and get it back on the right green carpet before tapping it in for triple par.

"Can you please check if there is a breeze over there?" he asked Riley straight-faced while he pointed his moist finger up into the sky trying to get a read on which way the wind was blowing.

"Oh, come on," Lisa said, looking at her watch. "Let's just putt out again," she told Emily and Riley shaking her head.

Scoops waited for two young girls to putt in front of him and then lined up for his shot.

"You'll never make it!" Riley yelled. "Just pick it up and forget it."

"Just pick it up?" Scoops gasped. "Champions don't just pick it up and go home!" Scoops pointed his putter at Riley. "Give up, geez, what if Columbus gave up and set sail for home?"

Riley laughed, "I bet Custer wished he'd gave up and went home."

"Not the same thing, Riley," he started his backswing "not the same thing."

Scoops topped the ball, and it popped out zinging by Lisa's head and crashing into a headless statue next to her.

"Scoops!" the girls screamed.

"Yikes!" Scoops shouted, "I think I knocked that guy's head off!"

"You almost knocked my head off, you idiot!" Lisa yelled, angrily at him. "You don't need to take a backswing when you're putting."

"Who did you learn that from," Scoops retorted, "Todd, in-between croquet, and lawn bowling lessons?"

"Let's just play nine holes," Lisa said, throwing up her hands. "This is going to take way too long."

"Soooooorry," Scoops drawled, "I just want to get my money's worth."

"Your money?" Riley repeated, smiling.

After what would have been a colossal meltdown if Scoops had played decent on any hole, the foursome made it to the ninth and final hole, aptly themed Rip Van Winkle.

"After this next group of five-year-olds play through, you can start, Scoops," Lisa said, putting an emphasis on five-year-olds.

"Sounds good," Scoops said oblivious to Lisa's subtle jab.

"Way to go!" a young mother yelled as she encouraged her little girl. "You got that in two."

"Yeah, yeah, hurry up," Scoops mumbled to himself as he lined up his putt. He looked up at Riley, "what's the score anyway?"

"They are at 36," he sighed, then finished some quick finger arithmetic. "We are at 72."

"Really?" Scoops said as if he was surprised, they were losing. "Wish Rhonda's bestie never found that pencil."

As if he was destined to redeem himself, Scoops inhaled deeply and took a swing as if he was trying to loft a lob wedge back over the gallery onto the green.

The four watched as Scoops bright pink ball bounced off Rip's boot and ricocheted off his hat. The four grimaced as if old Rip was finally going to lift his head finally awakening from his slumber. The ball continued rolling straight towards the hole.

Kerplunk!

"Hole in one!" Scoops yelled ecstatically in the direction of the little girl ahead of them as if he wanted to make sure she and her mother knew he beat her. He jumped up and down, "free game, I win a free game!"

Lisa lined up her shot behind him. "That's on the eighteenth hole Scoops, not the ninth," she sniveled.

Scoops was suddenly full of confidence. "Let's keep going, let's finish," he begged the group.

"Not a chance!" they replied all at once.

Go-Karts: 6:35 p.m.

"What's it like to be down 1-0 already champ?" Emily teased Riley as they made their way to the go-karts.

Riley nudged her on the shoulder.

"Did you just hit me?" she asked, serious as a judge.

"No, no, I didn't, well I guess, but no, I didn't mean, I wasn't thinking, I'm sorry..." Riley responded flustered.

"Just kidding," Emily laughed. "Wow Riley, I thought you were this trouble maker that was always up to no good."

"What do you mean?"

"I heard about your detention."

"You did?" Riley asked proudly. "How did you hear about that?"

"I just overheard Mr. Tillweed and Ms. Carpenter talking."

"What did they say?" Riley asked. She had piqued his interest.

"Nothing really," she continued. "Mr. Tillweed was just ranting about how his lip hurt because of your prank."

Riley laughed. "What a baby, did she kiss it better?"

"Yeah, what is with those two?" she frowned. "Who did they think they were fooling?"

"Mr. Wentworth, I guess," Riley replied. "I don't think he has a clue."

"I guess, well they don't have to worry about hiding it any more thanks to Scoops' discus skills."

Riley laughed, and then out of nowhere got outrageously courageous. "Do we?" he asked her, his voice shaking.

Emily smiled and brushed her blonde bangs out of her twinkling eyes, "I don't think so."

Riley's chest thundered. He wanted to jump up and down, but instead, he slowly reached and grabbed Emily's hand. She interlocked her fingers between his. He was so excited he could hardly breathe. If only he could freeze the moment forever.

"I am amazing at these," Scoops bragged to Lisa as they caught up to Riley and Emily.

"I am sure you are," Lisa replied, shaking her head again in disbelief. He was relentless. Neither of them noticed Emily and Riley holding hands as they continued to bicker back and forth like an old couple.

Scoops stopped abruptly, cupping his hand behind his ear. "Hey Lisa, do you hear that? I think they are playing our song?"

"We don't have a song, Scoops."

"Oh yeah," Scoops slumped, "we should."

Lisa rolled her eyes at Emily.

"You know, I am kind of like a melodic hook." Scoops went on.

"How so?"

"Well once I get in your head you can't get me out of it."

Lisa scoffed. "Yeah because you don't stop, it's just the same thing over and over. You are so obnoxious!"

"Really?" Scoops face saddened. "I always felt I was more like a good bass line. You know, one you hear, but you don't really notice, and soon you can't stop bobbing your head."

Lisa turned and stared him down with cold eyes. "I would equate you to a small bug, with tiny little legs, tiny little wings, that crawls into your ear canal and burrows into your eardrum. You can't get it out. It just sits in there wiggling its tiny little legs, flapping its tiny little wings, making you want to take whatever sharp object you can find and jam it into your ear. Not to kill the bug, because that won't erase the memory of the excruciating experience, but to kill yourself so can finally be free for good."

Emily and Riley stared at Lisa and Scoops slack-jawed waiting for Scoops to respond.

"Well, I think you're wonderful," Scoops softly whispered.

Lisa turned to Emily and Riley, palms up, jaw down. They were laughing hysterically. She made a fist at them and turned back to Scoops.

"How about a side pot then?" she suggested.

"Like what?"

"If I beat you, you tell my dad that you're sorry."

"And if I beat you?" Scoops asked. "Then what?"

"You can make fun of Todd."

Scoops laughed. "That is going to happen regardless. Let's up the ante. If you beat me, I will tell your dad I am sorry, and offer to clean his car, and if I win, you tell Todd to pound sand for at least a week and give me a chance."

She closed her eyes and sighed. "Alright, deal."

Emily whispered to Riley. "Scoops is in for it."

"Why is that?" Riley asked as he desperately tried to reach a mosquito biting him on the back with his free hand. There was no way he was letting go of Emily's hand to kill it with the other.

"Lisa has been driving go-karts and cars since she was born. Dr. Fiore is almost as nuts about racing as he is crazy about classical music."

"No, kidding," Riley smiled. "Sounds like Dr. Fiore better make himself an appointment with a good psychiatrist."

Emily laughed and threw his hand away to grab a helmet.

"Don't even think about going until the light turns green and keep it between the lines!" Chester shouted. Chester was about five foot four, six inches wide and had more tattoos than teeth. He could care less about his health but took his job as serious as the gospel truth. He wore an old green trucker hat and tucked his hair in behind his ears. "Brake into the turns, accelerate out of them!" he shouted as if he could hardly hear over the roaring engines of the tiny 50cc go-karts. "You're not driving Ferraris!"

"Really," Scoops mumbled as he walked passed him. "I thought these are what we drove over to get to the Ferraris, you know, like ship's tenders."

Chester heard him and didn't find it funny. He flipped a wad of chewing tobacco between his two teeth with his tongue and put his hand firmly against Scoops' chest. "Where are you going, buddy?"

Scoops looked down at his hand and slowly backed away.

Chester gestured at a nearby sign. "You taller?" he scowled.

Scoops laughed, "yes, in fact, I am pretty sure I do exceed the minimum height required." He looked at Riley as if they had just arrived on another planet. "By about a foot, maybe two."

Chester remained deadly serious. "Just making sure," he dropped his hand, "you may go."

Lisa, Emily, and Riley all passed him with no problem.

As Lisa hopped in her go-kart, Chester quickly rushed to help her. He was short of breath from the three long strides it took for him to get to her, so he took his time to speak. He stood over Lisa while he caught his wind, resting his sandal on her front tire. Chester's feet were filthy dirty and looked as though he had been raking asphalt all day.

"You are going to have to be careful on this here cart," he cautioned. "She gets going at a fairly good clip."

Lisa couldn't focus on anything but Chester's long toenails. *Speaking of a good clip*, she thought.

"Yep, I like your taste. This here kart is what I usually pick." He winked at her, almost stimulating her gag reflex. "You have made a darn good choice." He spit about a cup of tobacco juice on the ground beside her and then wiped his chin with the sleeve of his jean jacket.

"Thanks," Lisa said, her eyes quickly darting from his eyes to the spit, then back to his foot. Her pupils were transfixed on his toenails as if at any moment, he would try to slice her open.

"She is a sweet girl," Chester continued, slowly tapping his foot on the worn rubber wheel. "Not unlike yourself. She's easy on the eyes, hard on the ticker and soft and gentle on the curves."

Scoops had had enough. "Alright hillbilly, we're raring to go here, bud."

Chester just held up his arm and a finger as if to shush him. "If you need help at any point, just let me know," he gave Lisa a creepy eyebrow waggle.

Lisa looked like she was about to die.

Emily came to her rescue. "3-2-1 Go!" she yelled and hit the accelerator.

Riley roared after her so she couldn't get too far ahead.

"Hey!" Chester yelled, "Wait for the green light!" He just managed to step out of the way before Scoops gave him a pedicure with his left tire. He looked at Lisa as if they were fools for daring to disrespect the sport.

"Amateurs!" he said to her shaking his head. He brushed his long greasy hair behind his ears trying to play it cool. "No respect at all."

Lisa's eyes widened, and she clenched her teeth.

Chester anticipated what was coming and jumped out of the way just in time as Lisa pinned it.

Chester spent the next five to seven minutes shouting racing advice from the middle of the track as they zoomed around him. Only Lisa noticed him because she couldn't help it, she cringed every time he got within earshot. Emily and Riley were neck in neck. Neither of them wanted to pass each other. They just kept driving beside each other.

Staring into each other's eyes like an old couple in scooters at a nursing home. Scoops on-the-other-hand had nothing on his mind but the race. His knuckles were white as he gripped the steering wheel. The more his palms sweated, the harder he gripped the wheel. His right foot shook from holding down the gas pedal, but he didn't dare let it rest. He was determined to win.

Unfortunately, so was Lisa. When she lapped him for the third time, Scoops slammed his fists on the steering wheel. He took his eyes off the track only to see an all too familiar sight. Chester was running in the middle of the track, cheering on Lisa as she whizzed passed him.

"Come on!" he yelled as loud as he could, safe from Lisa hearing over the roar of the karts. "You have got to be kidding me!"

Chester's hat had long since blown off, but he could care less. His greasy hair stuck to his scalp as if held down by a whole bottle of hair gel.

As Lisa closed in on Scoops to lap him for the fourth time, he cranked his head to look at her. The sight of her smiling and waving drew the ire of the fiercest of competitors bottled up inside him.

"No, she isn't!" Scoops screamed. "Not this time!"

As he whipped around the final corner, Chester's hat blew in front of him like a tumbleweed skipping across a deserted highway. It startled him, causing him to overreact. He swerved to miss it like it was a doe caught in his headlights. As he did, he crossed over the forbidden yellow line and struck the used tires that lined the track with his front left tire, instantly propelling him into a spin. Lisa hit the brakes, but she was a split second too late. Her front bumper struck Scoops kart, and they both began to spin together as if locked in a heated salsa embrace.

As they twirled, Scoops couldn't take his eyes off Lisa. Her long dark hair blew across her face and gently kissed her soft cheeks. How he longed for her to reciprocate his love. Lisa stared back at him, yelling as they spun around in circles. Scoops couldn't hear her, but he could read her lips clearly.

"I'm going to kiss you!"

There it was. She was finally opening up to him. She was finally revealing to him how she felt. Suddenly, a completely peaceful moment came to a screeching halt. Both karts engines flooded with cheap watered down fuel and choked themselves out. As their karts came to rest, Scoops smiled blissfully at the love of his life who faced him head-on.

"I'm going to kill you!" she yelled, reaching for her seatbelt.

Scoops nodded peacefully like an enlightened monk. "Oh, kill."

"What did you think I was going to do you idiot?" she cried.

Chester was on the scene. "I told you to keep it between the lines, dude!" he shouted. "Are you alright, beautiful?" he asked, coming to Lisa's rescue as if he was a coast guardian saving an astronaut locked in an escape pod. He tried to help her get out of the kart, but nothing could have made Lisa move faster. She whipped off the seat belt and stormed off the track, turning to toss her helmet as hard as humanly possible at Chester as he chased after her.

The highs and lows were all too much for Scoops. He sat bewildered in his kart for about thirty seconds. Fortunately, for him, there was no risk for a post-accident kart explosion. When he got his wits about him, he jumped out of his kart to catch Lisa. First, he zigzagged through a row of tires as if he was at the NFL combine, then he skirted the long grass that fringed the track. As he was just about to hurdle the fence, he remembered he still had his helmet on. He quickly unbuckled it and hurled it at a dejected Chester who stood alone on the track, passionately sniffing up the scent of Lisa's hair from the inside of Lisa's sweaty helmet. With catlike reflexes, he blocked Scoops helmet with Lisa's as if he was in a heated game of dodgeball.

Surprised, and somewhat impressed, Scoops turned and continued after Lisa. "Wait!" Scoops yelled. "It was an accident!"

Scoops was still getting an earful when Emily and Riley walked up. "You guys, ok?" Riley asked.

"Yes," Lisa shot back, "but this moron almost killed me."

"Us," Scoops corrected her, "almost killed us."

"So now you admit it," she steamed.

"Yes, wouldn't that be the best way to go?" he asked dreamy-eyed. "You, me, a fiery go-kart crash, Shakespeare himself couldn't write a more tragic, but romantic ending."

Lisa looked at Emily. "Tell me you beat him," she demanded, pointing at Riley.

Riley and Emily looked at each other. Neither of them knew who had won. The truth was they had forgotten all about the race.

"Are you kidding?" she scowled at them. "You don't know?"

"Riley won," she quickly answered. "Yep beat me fair and square. It looks like we need a tie-breaker." A broad smile formed on her lips as if it was the best thing that could happen.

Forced to continue, Lisa let out a huge grunt that would have shamed a pig.

Arcade Free-For-All: 7:00 p.m.

"Have you ever considered not being such an incredibly big loser?" Lisa asked Scoops as they walked over to the token machine.

He looked back at her as if the thought had never crossed his mind. Inside it stung a little. "Nope, have you ever considered not being such a downer?"

Lisa scoffed, "your turn to pony up Scoops."

Scoops looked at Riley hopelessly, and then he began canvassing the room, "yeah, I just need to find a bank machine."

Riley and Emily giggled.

"Let's just each get our own tokens," Emily offered.

"Good idea," Riley agreed. "I will cover you, Scoops."

"Thanks, Riley." Scoops breathed a sigh of relief and then looked around, suggesting he was still trying to locate the nearest bank machine.

As they each took out ten dollars of tokens, Lisa stared at her watch and tapped her foot restlessly. "I have to go the bathroom," she announced to the group.

Emily immediately picked up the hint. "Me too."

When the girls were safely out of earshot, Scoops thanked Riley again for the tokens. "Sorry, Riley, I just don't have any money."

"Yeah, no problem," he slapped him on the shoulder. "You can owe me."

"Sounds good," Scoops replied. "One time, I tried to start learning about investing. You know, interest and stuff?"

"Yeah?"

"But they should really call it disinterest, talk about compound boredom. You know what I mean?"

"Yeah," Riley chuckled.

"Plus, I didn't have any money," Scoops admitted. "Kind of like learning to cook without any ingredients."

"Yeah."

"Or learning to skate without skates."

"I get it Scoops."

"Speaking of interest, or lack thereof, how is it going with Emily?" Scoops asked.

Riley's face glowed. "I am in love," he replied, giving his best Scoops impression. "And I think she is into me too!" Riley tried to keep his composure, but his excitement was pouring out of him. "We even held hands."

"Nice," Scoops mumbled. It was evident his thoughts had drifted off.

"How do you think it is going with Lisa?" Riley asked, flipping the conversation back on Scoops.

Scoops nodded confidently. "Pretty good," he paused, pursing his lips, "I think I have Lisa right where I want her."

They smiled.

Inside the bathroom, Lisa was fuming. "It is seven o'clock, Emily. My dad is going to be furious." She stared down at her phone. "Both my dad and Todd won't stop texting me."

"Yeah, they are probably out driving around looking for you." She chuckled to herself, "a real modern-day posse, arms dangling out the window, Beethoven cranked to eleven."

Lisa scowled back at her, "those boys are getting to you, aren't they?" She walked to the mirror to tie her hair up. "You even sound like them."

"Oh, come on, Lisa," Emily followed her and leaned against the counter. "They are refreshing. Do you honestly miss Todd?"

Lisa thought for a second. "Well, at least Todd has a plan."

"What plan? Rock you to sleep until you decide to marry him."

Lisa glared at her.

Emily sighed. "You are hard on Scoops, and you know it."

"No, I am not!" she shouted back denying the obvious.

"You know what I think? I think you are falling for him, and you're scared."

"Ha!" Lisa scoffed, "Yeah okay."

"No, I think you are. I saw you a few times today. You were enjoying yourself, Mona Lisa."

Lisa smiled, her voice softened. "How dare you call me that?" As she walked out of the bathroom, she gently shoved Emily. It was just a subtle enough hint to let Emily know she was right.

"When the clock on the wall says 7:10 we all will have up to 15 minutes, and 15 minutes only to get as many tickets as possible. Or if you run out of tokens before then, you are done," Riley explained to the other three contestants. "The most tickets at the end wins another date."

"Or not another date," Lisa chimed in.

"Unlikely," Scoops quickly responded.

The four stared at the clock as the second arm closed in on 12. "Ready… go!" Riley shouted.

Scoops instantly ran off. Lisa took off in the exact opposite direction.

Emily grabbed Riley's arm, and they casually sauntered off together.

15 Minutes Left

"What do you want to try first?" Emily asked Riley.

"Well, I liked that hand holding thing we tried earlier, but I guess if you want to move to kissing, we can always try that."

"Funny, I meant games."

"Well," Riley responded, disappointed the kiss didn't make the cut. "Skee-Ball?"

"Too cliché."

"Hmmm," Riley looked around the arcade. "How about Feed Big Bertha?"

"What's that?" she asked, unsure if she should be offended or not.

"You know," Riley answered as if she had played it a thousand times before. "The one that you throw as many balls into Bertha's mouth as possible."

"No, I don't know."

"Really?" Riley asked, surprised. "It's a classic."

She laughed.

"That's like saying you have never watched Star Wars."

"Is it?" Emily rolled her eyes.

"Let's play," Riley said, pointing to a large creepy cloth doll with scarlet red hair.

Emily hesitated. "I guess, but you go first."

"No problem, I'll show you how to do it," Riley said with confidence. "Now what you do is you throw as many balls as possible in her mouth in thirty seconds. Each one you get in makes her gain weight. The more weight, the more tickets rewarded."

"How do you know all this?" she asked with a look of disgust. She looked around as if someone might be watching them.

Riley caught on that Emily might not be entirely behind the idea of throwing red balls in a woman's mouth to help her pack on the pounds. "Well," he said thoughtfully. "I think it has an inspirational message."

Emily looked at him in disbelief. "What's that?"

"Well, I think we should always encourage women to feel comfortable with how they look regardless of how much they eat. Instead, our society pressures them into being thin all the time." Riley dropped a coin in the machine. "It's quite sad."

Emily rolled her eyes. "Well, she is not feeding herself. You are stuffing food in her mouth."

"Yeah, that is what I am saying. That's how bad it has got. Girls won't even feed themselves anymore."

The balls released, and the clock started counting down. Riley grabbed a couple of balls in both hands and started whipping them at Bertha's mouth. "Eat, Bertha eat!" he shouted. 275-300-325, with every ball Bertha gained twenty-five pounds.

Emily laughed. "Oh my gosh, her stomach is getting bigger."

"That's okay," Riley cried. "We are okay with that. Look how happy she is. Chew Bertha chew!"

"This is so awful," Emily said, covering her eyes, but under her wrists, she hid a wide smile. "Time's up," she announced peeking through her fingers. "Thank goodness for Bertha."

Riley was ecstatic, "Look at all these tickets!" He reached down and started to collect them. "More, more, more!" he yelled like a ten-year-old as they spilled out of the machine.

"How many?" she asked

"Too many," Riley said wide-eyed as he held the tickets in the palm of his hands as if he held a pan full of gold.

Emily shook her head, unimpressed. "You want me to show you how to do it?"

"You wouldn't," Riley said quickly changing his stance on the morality of the game. "You mean you're going to get off your soap box and contribute to world's obesity epidemic?"

They both turned to look at Big Bertha. Her stomach had shrunk back to its normal size.

"Oh," Riley said to Emily, his face darkening. "That is quite upsetting."

"What?"

"I think Bertha is bulimic."

Emily laughed and hit Riley on the shoulder. "Riley that is not something to joke about."

"No. You're right, this game is awful. There are no good messages in this game that contribute to the greater social good."

Emily dropped in a coin and started throwing balls into big Bertha's gaping mouth. "Eat Bertha, eat!"

Riley watched her as she hurled red ball after red ball in Bertha's mouth. 300-325-350. "Whoa," he cried, "don't try too hard, or you won't get that date."

Emily smiled at Riley and picked up the pace. "Eat Bertha, eat!"

Riley laughed and started picking up balls to help her.

"What are you doing?" Emily asked as Bertha swallowed another two balls.

"I might as well help feed her," Riley added two more balls. "She's just going to puke them up anyway."

By the entrance to the arcade, Lisa was ignoring a group of tweens who were begging for a turn on Big Bass Wheel Pro. She was going for the 5,000-ticket jackpot, and no one was going to get in her way. She had done quite well at Cyclone pulling in two major scores, but the 5,000 tickets that flashed above the big wheel called to her like a mirage in the middle of an arid desert. Tickets hung around her neck like beaver pelts on a trapper, and nothing could quench her thirst for more.

Scoops was nowhere in sight.

10 Minutes Left

By the third game of Feed Big Bertha, Emily was starting to lose interest but was still enjoying watching Riley try to beat his high score. She leaned against the game and watched him continue to throw balls with his tongue dangling out. As she watched him, she began to reflect on her relationship with Randle. She had spent countless hours with him, mostly because of Lisa and Todd, and in just a couple short days, she felt herself already falling hard for Riley.

At the risk of disclosing her feelings, she started a discussion about Lisa and Scoops. "Scoops likes Lisa a lot, doesn't he?"

"Yep," Riley answered frankly. There was no point in denying the obvious. "Does she like him?"

"I don't know?"

Riley called upon every sales skill he had and prepared to go full bore into pitch mode. "What's not to like?" he asked.

Emily laughed. She looked to the ceiling as if she was going to start reciting the alphabet backward. "He is a character, isn't he?"

"Yep," Riley confirmed. There was no denying that, either. Riley cheered as he ripped off another long thread of tickets. "Your turn."

"I'm good," Emily responded.

"Your loss," he said, plopping in another token.

Bertha immediately started devouring plastic red balls.

"It's too bad about his dad," Emily lamented.

"Who's dad?" Riley asked, still not paying full attention to what she was saying.

"Scoops," she replied softly.

"What about him?" Riley said. "Come on!" he yelled at the balls to return faster.

"You don't know?" Emily asked, surprised.

"Know what?"

Emily stopped leaning on the game. "Maybe I shouldn't say anything. I thought you knew."

"Knew what?" Riley asked again. He stopped throwing balls and looked at Emily. "What did you hear?" He threw the last ball in his hand.

Emily realized she had gone too far to stop now. "Well, promise not to tell or say anything?"

"For sure."

She hesitated. "I really shouldn't."

"Emily," Riley said sternly.

"Well," she continued, "Scoops' mom is helping clean my dad's clinic in the evenings. Last night I was showing her what to clean, and we started talking. She was worried about him because over the last six months he has gone from having good grades to causing the Principal to call home two days in a row."

"You know Scoops' mom?" Riley's eyes narrowed. "Wait, is he an honours student?"

Emily laughed.

"Does he know you know his mom?"

"I don't think so."

"What else did she say? What about his dad?"

"Well, they just moved here."

"I know that," Riley said, growing impatient.

Emily let her eyes drift from Riley's. "Because his dad died."

"What?" Riley gasped. His mouth dropped open.

She continued. "His dad died last month of cancer, so they moved here to get a new start. She said it has been tough on him. I can hardly imagine."

"Are you kidding me?" Riley said, turning around and sitting down on the machine as the timer ticked down to zero.

"No, sorry," she said softly, "he didn't tell you?"

"Well no," Riley rubbed at his eye, "it hasn't come up."

"Sorry, Riley," Emily said sympathetically. "I thought you knew."

"I need to sit down," Riley said, his voice shaken. He started walking to a nearby table.

As they walked away, Feed Big Bertha churned out two abandoned tickets.

5 Minutes Left

As Riley and Emily sat together at a table, Lisa walked up to them proudly displaying her tickets draped across her arms like a fresh kill.

"Really," Riley said wide-eyed, "how many tickets do you have?"

Lisa ignored him, waiting for Emily to divulge how many tickets she had won.

"Nice, Lisa," Emily congratulated her.

"Why are you guys just sitting here?" Lisa asked.

"Just taking a break," Emily replied, worried Lisa might notice Riley's somber mood.

Riley didn't need the help. "Arms are sore, Lisa," he said, waving his throwing arm in a circle as if he was just stepping off the pitcher's mound. "Bertha could pack it in there."

171

Just then, Scoops dragged himself up to the table. He looked exhausted.

"What happened to you, Randle?" Riley teased him, "the 200-meter dash 195 meters too long?"

Scoops smiled, appreciating the 'Randle' burn but didn't waste the breath to laugh or respond. He flopped into a chair and dropped forward landing face first on the table, his arms stretched out before him.

"You okay buddy?" Riley asked again.

Scoops mumbled something, but with his lips pressed against the table, no one could understand his muffled voice.

"Sorry, can't hear you," Riley said.

Scoops lifted his head off the table, shooting Riley a death glare. "I said, Dance Dance Revolution."

"Dance Dance Revolution?" Lisa echoed.

"Yeah, I played it like ten times," Scoops exhaled.

"That game doesn't give tickets," Riley revealed.

Scoops managed to push himself back on his feet slowly, but left his hands on the desk and leaned down face-to-face with Riley as if he was a teacher standing over a student's desk. "Yes, I realize that now!" he growled.

Riley and Emily burst out laughing. Even Lisa cracked a smile.

When they finally got their wits about them, Riley stood up and looked at the clock.

"Five minutes left."

"You guys might as well give up," Lisa said.

"No way!" Scoops said as if he was about to lead his Company out of the trenches. "Not today, Lisa, today we will stand and fight."

"Tonight," Lisa pointed out. "Tonight." She looked at her phone. "I have to go home."

"One more game," Riley decreed, no was not an option.

"What game?" Emily asked. "Please, not Big Bertha."

Riley stood up and stared across the room as if the bright lights of heaven were beacons leading him home. "There it is," he stated and pointed across the room as if he was Lewis or Clark looking out over the Pacific Ocean.

The three friends followed his finger.

"Jumping Jackpot?" Emily asked.

"No," Riley smiled steely-eyed. "Spin-N-Win!"

Scoops shouted, "Yes, I love that game!" He jumped in the air. "I am awesome at it!"

Riley didn't even look at him. "I'm sure you are Scoops. I'm sure you are."

When the four reached the game, Scoops broke into a thorough but unnecessary tutorial. "Ok, so what you have to do is pull the big lever. The wheel will start to spin. As you can see, the wheel has a bunch of numbers on it."

Lisa wasn't listening. She was already counting her tickets.

"What you want is for the wheel to stop on the highest number," Scoops advised. "I suggest 1,000."

"Thanks for the insider info," Lisa jeered, still counting the heap of tickets in her hands. "How many tickets do you have Emily?" she asked. "I think I have enough to win already."

Riley shook his head, vehemently. "No way, no counting tickets until the end."

Scoops jumped in nodding as if he was the second referee verifying a call. "Yep, those are the rules."

Lisa responded by dropping her shoulders and letting out an angry sigh.

Time's Up

Spin-N-Win proved much more difficult than it looked. None of the four managed to land on a number higher than 40. They walked up to the ticket-counting machine, and Lisa immediately started feeding in her tickets. 50 tickets, 75 tickets, seven tickets. She kept going and going, pulling tickets from everywhere.

"277 tickets," she proudly announced as she read the final total. "You're up, Emily." Then she resumed staring intently at her phone.

Emily started inserting her tickets. Five tickets, 15 tickets, ten tickets.

"30 tickets," Emily said enthused.

"Nice," Riley said, congratulating her.

"30 tickets?" Lisa howled. "Are you kidding me right now? What were you doing?"

"Okay, you guys have 307 tickets. That is going to be hard to beat," Riley stated as he began feeding his tickets into the counter.

"165," he read, shaking his head disappointed.

"Good job, Riley," Emily consoled him and patted him gently on the back.

Lisa rolled her eyes.

"My turn," Scoops said as he stepped up to the machine. He opened his fist, revealing a handful of separated tickets. He started feeding them into the machine one by one.

"Are you serious right now?" Lisa erupted. "Who rips their tickets? What are you an aspiring carnie? I don't have time for this," she snorted. "I have to go!"

"Relax, I am hurrying," Scoops said calmly, but obviously wasn't in any panic at all. He meticulously fed each ticket in as if they might get stuck if he wasn't careful.

"Let's go!" she barked at Emily.

Emily didn't budge. She looked at Riley and sighed. "Sorry, looks like no date for you."

"Come on?" Riley pleaded. He glared at Lisa as if her level of effort correlated directly to how bad she wanted to sabotage his happiness.

Scoops had disappeared.

"A deal is a deal," Lisa said, coldly.

"Well maybe we can make an exception," Emily suggested. Her eyes begged Lisa to reconsider.

"Absolutely not!" Lisa dictated as she looked around urgently. "Where is he now?"

As if she had called him, Scoops came out of nowhere.

"Where did you go now, Scoops?" she snarled. "Back to win more tickets from Dance Dance Revolution?"

He ignored her. "I got this for you," he said, holding his hand out like a timid child offering oats to a wild mare. "I figured you won fair and square and I wanted to pick a nice prize for you." He opened his fist, and inside his sweaty palm was a small plastic ring. "I think you will wear it beautifully."

Lisa looked at it and didn't know what to say. Scoops was being serious for once.

"That is so sweet, Scoops," Emily praised.

"Thanks, Emily," he said. "It's Sleeping Beauty."

"Why because I am so boring?" Lisa said, putting her guard up. Expecting an insult to follow shortly.

"Lisa," Emily said disapprovingly.

"No, because you are beautiful," Scoops replied admiringly.

Lisa warmed up for the first time in over an hour. "Well, thanks, Scoops."

"And…" Scoops started to continue. "Since Todd has lulled you to sleep…"

"What?" Lisa interjected, cutting him off before he could finish.

Scoops had no intention of stopping, and everybody braced for it.

"—sleep," Scoops waded in, "I was hoping that one day, I could be the handsome prince that wakes you up."

Lisa's eyes sparkled. Her walls started to come crashing down. Before she let him know he had wedged a foot in the door of her heart, she turned to look at Riley and Emily. They both were staring at her glossy eyed.

"So…" Riley asked Lisa, grabbing Emily's hand as if he was afraid the girls were going to walk out of Bridgeport Fun Park and be gone forever.

Lisa looked back at Scoops whose eyes were wide with anticipation. Her face broke into a broad smile. "We will give you one more chance tomorrow, but this time, we get to pick the place."

Emily couldn't hold in her excitement. "Yes!" she yelled joyfully. "Great idea, Lisa, and you boys have to dress up."

"What kind of dress up?" the boys chorused.

"Like fancy!"

"Fancy, I don't have anything fancy?" Scoops said as he pulled at his tattered sweater. "I don't even know what fancy is."

"Well, you better find something," Emily said, and she leaned in and gave Riley a soft kiss on the cheek.

Riley's beamed, just catching his balance before he fell over.

Lisa stuck her tongue out, "yuk."

Scoops leaned forward expectantly, waiting for his turn.

"You're dreaming Scoops. I will ask my dad when he wants his car cleaned. See you tomorrow." She snubbed him and walked off.

Emily wished the boys goodnight before chasing after Lisa. Just before she reached the exit, she stopped and pulled a stack of tokens from her faded jeans and gave them to a little curly haired boy.

14
CONFESSIONS

Riley was sure he wasn't going to be able to sleep all night. When he finally got home, it was close to 9:00 p.m. It must have been Scoops' great impression or his own jovial mood, but somehow his parents let him off the hook for coming home so late. It was a little unorthodox that they didn't meet him with a barrage of the Kushinski classic questions. Where were you? Who were you with? Who are his parents again? What is he planning on doing after graduation? Mr. Kushinski knew that he and Scoops had wandered off with two very attractive young girls, and by now, Riley was sure that his mom had a detailed briefing. There were no secrets in the Kushinski household.

He made his way quickly up the stairs to his room, so his presence didn't evoke any form of discussion and to ensure he was clearly out of harm's way in case the ceasefire was called off. Just as he flopped back on his bed, reliving the best day of his life, Charlotte barged into the room in her butterfly pajamas. She was obviously unaware there was a question injunction.

"How was track today, Riley?" she asked as she plopped down beside him. No salutation was necessary.

Riley grunted.

"How did Jack do?" She was clearly not interested in her big brother's performance.

Riley dove deeper into caveman mode, grunting even louder.

"Wish I could have been there," she said dreamy-eyed. Then her face turned deathly serious. "Dad said you and Jack left early with two girls." She sat up and looked down at her brother. "Who were they?"

Riley opened one eye and looked at his little sister. In a split second, she had turned from a frenetic adolescent teen with Scoopmania to a jealous wife about to hire a hitman to kill her unfaithful husband.

"Just friends," he said as he pushed himself up off the mattress and made his way out of his room down the hall to the bathroom. Charlotte hopped after him like a bear cub trying to keep up with its mother.

"What is her name?" she pressed.

Riley reached for his toothbrush. "Emily."

"I hate Emily," she said matter-of-factly as she sat down on the edge of the bathtub.

"Why?" Riley gurgled.

"I just do," she dolefully replied. "Do you remember my favourite movie, Titanic? I've finally found my Jack."

Riley spat in the sink. "All I remember is that annoying song you and mom play all the time."

Charlotte closed her eyes and smiled as if she was replaying the song in her head. "My Heart Will Go On, I love Celine Dion, I love that song, that movie." She sighed heavily, "I love Jack."

"Doesn't he die in the end?"

Charlotte ignored him. "I just can't bear to think about Jack with anyone else."

"Get a grip," Riley blurted, toothpaste bubbles flying everywhere. He spat and almost considered flossing but then thought better of it. "I am sure your heart will go on, you're half his age."

"Am not!" she protested.

Riley wiped his mouth. "Arg," he grumbled, "you even sound like him." He thought about washing his face, but he occasionally caught the scent of Emily's perfume and didn't want to lose it.

"Really, I sound like him?" she replied beaming. "I think we would make a great couple." She went on longingly, "he is so cute, we talk the same, mom and dad seem to love him…" she paused, her face darkened. "Now, I just need to get rid of Emily."

"Lisa," Riley corrected her as he left the bathroom and made his way back to his room.

Charlotte followed Riley as if she had him on a leash. "Who's Lisa?" She stopped dead in her tracks, her expression withering. "Wait, there are two girls?"

Riley pulled his curtains closed and turned to look at her. "No, I like Emily, he likes Lisa."

She breathed a sigh of relief. Then she replayed Riley's statement in her mind. "Wait, he likes her?"

Riley walked across his room and switched the light off. "I think so."

"Oh," she said solemnly, "does she like him?"

Riley sighed as he knelt beside his bed to thank God for putting Emily in his life. "I don't think so."

It was music to Charlotte's ears. "Great!" she cheered and leaned in to give him a goodnight kiss.

Riley pulled away to protect his hallowed cheek, but she was too quick.

"Love you!" she yelled as she scampered out of the room, just in time to hear her dad yell from downstairs.

"Charlotte, bed!"

Riley wasn't as thrilled. Charlotte's interrogation had caused him to think about Scoops rather than replaying his pleasant memories of himself and Emily. Instead, he tried to recollect every exchange between Scoops and Lisa. It was true. He wasn't sure Lisa reciprocated Scoops' feelings, which weighed even heavier on his mind as he recollected his conversation with Emily about Scoops' father. It nagged at him how Lisa had treated Scoops, albeit somewhat deservingly so.

He tried to turn his mind off Scoops and Lisa and back on Emily. As Riley lay in the dark staring at the ceiling, he scrunched up his nose and tried to sniff out her scent on his cheek. To his dismay, all he could smell was his little sister's bubblegum toothpaste.

Riley and Scoops had agreed to meet at Starbucks on the corner of 5th and Weber at 9:30 a.m. sharp. It was a trendy little spot just on the outskirts of the downtown entertainment district. Riley had heard of a small store they could rent tuxedos. The girls had one condition they were obligated to meet for them to see them again, and Riley and Scoops were going to make sure they didn't breach the agreement on a technicality.

Riley sat, and people watched from a small patio sipping on a tall house blend because it was all he could afford. He had saturated it with cream and sugar.

Scoops strolled up fifteen minutes late as though he had been held up in a slow department store checkout line. "This place is crazy!" he said, looking around as if he was in Times Square on New Year's Eve.

Riley looked around as if he was missing something. "What are you talking about? I think I can hear wind chimes from two blocks away," he exaggerated.

Scoops put his hands on his hips and looked down at Riley. "This is a pretty affluent neighbourhood."

Riley was surprised again, by what Scoops knew and didn't know.

"You look like a real hipster," Scoops remarked.

Riley looked down at what he was wearing. He had on the same thing as the day before. "What do you mean by that?"

"You know, just sitting here, at Starbucks, on the patio, Saturday morning drinking your macchiato or whatever you have there."

"Coffee."

Scoops eyes sunk a little bit as if a simple coffee had just debunked his whole theory. "Having a coffee, being all hipster like." He sat down next to Riley. "Mind if I join you? I know lots of interesting things about theatre, trees, and climate change, you know."

Riley chuckled. "You do?"

Scoops face got serious. "Yeah, I do. You do realize the weather changes four times a year in some other parts of the world. Even turns the leaves."

Riley nodded knowingly, "the four seasons."

Scoops corrected him. "Nope, that is a hotel. I stayed there once. It was the same temperature the whole time."

Riley wasn't interested in playing this game today. "You want coffee?"

"Don't touch the stuff," Scoops said sharply. "Makes me jumpy." He scanned around the patio as if he had already been sitting too long and had to move on. "Where is this tux place?"

"Just down the street at the next corner."

"How far is that?"

Riley frowned at him, "the next corner, so... a block."

Scoops bolted out of his chair as if he had just taken a shot of espresso. "Let's go then."

"Wait," Riley insisted. "Sit down. I want to talk to you about something."

Scoops sighed, sensing the seriousness in Riley's voice. Nevertheless, he obliged his friend and sat back down. "What?"

Riley didn't know how to start, so he just jumped right in the deep end prepared to tread water. "I heard about your dad?"

"From who," Scoops asked. "Your dad?"

"No," Riley quickly replied, and then his eyes narrowed, "wait, my dad knows?"

Scoops paused thoughtfully. Maybe they were talking about two different things, and the lawyer lie was still in play. "Something happen at the office?"

"Scoops, I know your dad doesn't work with my dad," Riley said. "Emily told me."

Scoops was relieved Mr. Kushinski hadn't breached his trust. He had been a light in a dimly lit tunnel. Not exactly the exit but letting him know he was going the right way. He held that close to him. "Emily?" he asked curiously.

"Yeah, I guess she works with your mom."

Scoops recalled his mother's note about the clinic, the daughter showing her the ropes. "Ah," he breathed.

"I'm sorry, Scoops," Riley said sympathetically. "But you should have told me."

"Why?" he asked, defensively. "What difference would it have made?"

"Well, none I guess," Riley couldn't think of a better answer.

"That is why I didn't." Scoops jumped back up to his feet. "Let's go."

Riley looked up at him. "Well, do you want to talk about it?"

"Does it look like I want to talk about it?" Scoops said, swinging his arms as if he was pretending to walk away. "We got a big date tonight, man."

Riley wasn't one to shy away from an awkward conversation, and he knew somewhere hidden deep inside, Scoops was suppressing his true feelings and needed to let them out. "What was he like?" he asked.

Scoops' smile vanished. His shoulders sagged, and he sat back down slowly. He knew he couldn't avoid the topic any longer. "My dad was an exceptional man," he said with deep fervor.

Riley waited for him to continue, but he didn't. Riley watched as Scoops sat silently in private reflection.

When he was ready, Scoops spoke. "He wasn't a lawyer."

Riley chuckled.

"He worked for our town's Parks and Recreation Department."

Riley just nodded letting Scoops continue.

"Everybody important to him loved him, which made him the happiest person in the world. He was always positive and could find the silver lining in everything."

"Sounds like a great guy."

"He knew what mattered you know? He put his life into my mom, to me. We didn't have much, but we had him, you know what I mean? He even took a job that no one else would want. A job that people would think was beneath them, just to be close to us, just to be home with us every night."

Riley had never seen Scoops so open, so vulnerable, so still.

"You know what he did, Riley?" Scoops asked, his eyes beginning to water.

"Parks and rec for the town."

"No, like what he did, did."

"What do you mean?"

"He scooped up poo, garbage, and cleaned bathrooms. His biggest workplace hazard was stepping in a steaming hot load of canine feces, and his most pressing issue was if a port-a-potty was out of toilet paper.

He took abuse from people for it too. People walked all over him and didn't understand that all that mattered to him was keeping those close to him happy. He pretended it didn't hurt, but I know it did."

Riley sat straight-faced. Hanging on every word as Scoops continued to unveil every detail about his father.

"I didn't understand, I loved him for it and hated him for it at the same time. I was embarrassed. I swore to myself I would never let people walk on me. I put everything I had into getting top marks, thinking I needed to amount to something better. I had no friends, and I was completely self-centered. I looked at everyone as a rung in a ladder I needed to climb higher."

Riley found his honesty surprising and at the same time, refreshing. "There is nothing wrong with being a straight A student and trying to be successful."

"Yeah, but there is with being a selfish, pompous and ungrateful jerk," Scoops shot back.

"Scoops," Riley said, "you're not—"

Scoops cut him off, "name is actually Jack."

"I know," Riley said, smiling. "This, I hear."

Scoops rested his elbows on his knees and stared across the street. He continued sharing while he had the courage. "When he died, I vowed to stop worrying about impressing people and letting my goals, accomplishments, and failures define me. Life is too short. I want to fill this life with as many good memories with those close to me as I can and have no shame or regrets. Love, be loved and encourage others to love. That is a legacy I can die happy with too."

Riley had opened a vault that Scoops had locked. Now that it was open, he was going to get it out so he could seal it shut again.

"Scoops," he murmured. "That is why I want to be called Scoops."

Riley was confused. "What are you talking about?"

"I want to be called Scoops as a constant reminder of my father. No one really knew he was there, but he always made people happy, even if they didn't realize it at the time."

Well, you are kind of hard not to notice, Riley thought, but he wisely kept it to himself.

"I'm going to follow his example but with one minor tweak." Scoops ran his fingers through his hair and smirked at Riley. "I'm not going to get trampled on. Whatever I am doing, whatever is going on, I am going to make the best of it and not let anyone get in the way. That means never telling someone something they want to hear just to win them over or not telling someone something they don't want to hear just to keep them happy and let them get away with something they shouldn't. If someone wants to be a jerk like I was, to people close to me or me, I won't be shy when it comes to letting them know."

Riley was at a loss for words. Never in a million years did he expect this. Scoops, including his peculiar name, finally completely made sense.

"Just one minor tweak?" Riley teased him and laughed. "You're a real beauty Scoops."

Scoops ignored the compliment. "Keep this to yourself, alright," he said firmly. "I don't want any of this getting out. It will ruin my reputation of being just another bratty teenager."

"I get it," Riley reassured him. "Remember what is important and never let someone else put your spirits in the red."

They both smiled and stood up from the table. They started walking down the street towards the tuxedo shop, leaving behind a half-full cup of coffee on the table.

15
TUX MAN

The sandwich board on the sidewalk promised the men's formal wear store carried all the top brands and latest fashions. Riley read aloud an additional sign on the door, "serving both the fashion-forward and conservative dresser."

"What are we?" Scoops asked, looking at their reflections in the window. Nothing they wore suggested that they deserved any accolades for their sense of style.

Riley bit his lip and nodded his head, admiring his wardrobe. "Definitely fashion forward."

"That is what I was thinking," Scoops agreed.

As they walked into the store, they collided with a draft of cold air.

"Jeepers," Scoops said shivering, expecting to see curing meat hanging from the racks instead of suits.

"Can I help you?" An eerie voice carried from behind a stack of folded sweaters.

The boy's heads turned in the direction of the sound trying to get a glimpse of its origin. A gaunt man stepped out from behind a tie rack about ten paces from the sweaters. Startled, and even more confused, the boys looked at each other, trying to determine how the man had managed to get from the sweaters to neckties so quickly. He approached them methodically like a lion stalking his prey. Regardless of how quick he was in the shadows, in plain sight, he moved in super slow motion.

"We're just looking," Scoops shouted as if to alert witnesses of their whereabouts in case they mysteriously disappeared in the next few minutes.

The man eyed the boys as if he was about to pounce. "Just looking?" he said. His frown turned into an icy stare as he ran his wiry fingers up and down a measuring tape wrapped around his neck like a necklace. "What are you looking to find?"

Riley looked at Scoops as if they had just walked into a toolshed in Texas and caught Leatherface sharpening a chainsaw.

Scoops discretely pointed to a large sign over the cashier that read, Friendly, Experienced Service. "What about creepy?" he whispered, his voice shaking.

Riley shushed him as the quiet man stared them down with dark, sunken eyes.

The man turned and walked away as slowly as he appeared, tucking his shirt into his loosely fitting slacks as he went. Nothing he wore implied he could help them source what they were looking for, and there was obviously no policy on wearing store merchandise.

"Well, actually," Riley called after him.

Scoops was shaking his head at Riley, screaming NO!

Riley ignored him. "We are looking to rent a couple of tuxes for the evening."

The man twirled around instantly to face them, his body contorting as he spun on his heels. His eyes were wide and mouth open as if he just received the heart after watching a human sacrifice. He raised his arms grimacing as if he was holding two heavy jugs of water and softly whispered, "Well, then have a look around." He turned around slowly and disappeared behind a rack of suit coats.

"Let's make a run for it," Scoops blurted as soon as the man was out of sight. "This guy gives me the heebie-jeebies."

"And miss our date with the girls? Do you know of any other places we can get a tux?"

"I don't care. It looks like he stole these tuxes from corpses. The guy is obviously a grave robber."

"Come on, he is not that bad."

"Are you kidding me right now? I feel like I just walked into a horror movie." Scoops was all about flight, not fight. "Let's get out while we can!"

Riley played to his conscience. "What did you just say about loving everyone? Give him a chance. He hasn't done anything yet."

Scoops face dropped and he sighed heavily. "Ah, you are right."

The man cleared his throat behind them. He had obviously heard their entire discussion.

Startled, Scoops almost jumped into Riley's arms.

"Having trouble finding what you are looking for?"

Riley mocked Scoops doing his best Shaggy, "Like, yeah, we are looking for like, some tuxes."

"Well, we have lots of styles," the man responded. "I can dig up a few options for you."

"Dig up?" Scoops gasped. "I'm sure you will." Scoops wasn't interested in spending all day with this serial killer. "We'll just take your most popular rental."

"Oh," the man said disappointedly. "Well, in that case. That makes things quite simple. Let's just get your measurements."

He raised his tape up to Scoops shoulder.

Scoops looked back at him as if he was Buffalo Bill trying to find the perfect piece of flesh to complete his women suit. "No thanks," he said petrified, swatting at him as he backed away.

"Excuse me?"

"No thanks, I am good." Scoops stuttered.

Riley interjected. "Come on, Scoops. It needs to fit."

"Well, his doesn't fit," Scoops protested, pointing at the starving man's outfit. "This guy doesn't need a belt to hold up his pants. He needs a full Scouts troop with a bundle of tent poles."

The man looked terribly offended. "Excuse me?"

"Well come on, when is the last time you measured yourself?"

"Well, I…" the man stammered.

"At least two of you ago," Scoops suggested.

Riley tried to make up for his friend. "Listen, sorry, Mr.," he paused, "sorry, I didn't catch your name."

"Hans," the man replied. "The name is Hans."

Scoops gasped. "Hans. What is that short for, Hannibal?"

The puzzled man looked at Scoops, "It is short for Johannes."

"Like the composer," Riley said. "Hans Zimmer."

"Why yes," Hans replied. He looked at Riley, one eyebrow raised. "Do you like classical music?"

Scoops interrupted them. "I hate music!" he shouted in the man's face as if his admission would have them kicked out of the store.

Hans and Riley ignored him.

"Yes, I do," Riley said.

Their newfound bond, as much of a façade as it was turned the attention off Scoops. Riley and Hans walked to the mirror at the back of the store to take measurements. Scoops stayed where he was so he could still see the door. In a few minutes, Riley came back in a black tuxedo, white shirt, and black bow tie. He looked sharp.

"How do I look?" he asked Scoops.

"Alive."

Riley just rolled his eyes. "Okay, your turn."

Scoops waned like an infant getting their second needle. "Do I have to?"

"Think of Lisa."

"Alright," Scoops said with newfound bravery. "But if I'm not back in five minutes…"

Riley smiled, "just wait a bit longer?"

"No, heck no!" Scoops shouted, grabbing and shaking Riley by the shoulders. "Get back there and drag me out of here before I become a pocket square in his wardrobe of human flesh!"

Hans was once again standing directly behind Scoops. He coughed nonchalantly. Scoops turned slowly. His lips clasped tightly together, shame-faced.

"You ready?" Hans asked Scoops.

"Yep," he said, popping his lips. He turned to Riley, "I will tell you about the rest of the movie later. Anyway, it's really funny. Hilarious actually, could never happen in real life."

Five minutes later, Scoops came out of the back unscathed. Hans lingered close behind.

"Wow, buddy," Riley said approvingly. "Looking dapper, Lisa is going to love it."

"Who is Lisa?" Hans asked.

"No one," Scoops quickly responded as if there was still time to protect his family and friends. Hans and Scoops had obviously not been able to connect in the same way Hans and Riley did.

Hans had given up. He floated effortlessly like a wraith to the checkout counter. "How will you be paying for this?"

Scoops patted the pockets of his tuxedo as if he had somehow misplaced his wallet in it at some point before entering the store.

Riley looked at Hans. "I got it. Let me just change back into my clothes, and I will grab it."

"You don't have to," Scoops said.

Riley just looked at him and then at Hans smiling, "yeah I do."

Hans reciprocated with a crooked smile of his own, "a real gem of a pal you got."

"You're a gem!" Scoops recoiled. Although it was unintentional, it was the nicest thing Scoops said to Hans all morning.

16
IMPLOSION

Riley and Scoops were safe in the Kushinski's backyard. The smell of fresh baked cookies wafted out of the window across the lawn to where Riley was firing tennis balls at Scoops. They played on a small asphalt pad originally intended for shooting hoops, not for hockey, but the rim had been ripped off for years. Scoops had volunteered to play net because, well, he was awesome at it. So far, the posts had saved more shots than Scoops. He had a Louisville goal stick in his right hand and in his left hand, he wore an old worn-out baseball mitt. Regardless of where Riley shot, Scoops made sure he flashed the leather every time. Riley considered firing a snapshot high glove side, but thought better of it. He knew he wouldn't be able to stand Scoops if he actually caught it and ran around the yard pretending he had just made the play of the year.

"Where do you think they are going to take us tonight?" Riley asked Scoops.

"Hopefully somewhere a bit classier than Bridgeport Fun Park," Scoops answered. "Otherwise, we are going stand out like Todd in an etiquette class."

Riley laughed. "Yeah, I can't stand those guys."

Just the thought of them angered Riley, and he put a little extra torque behind his slap shot.

The ball caught Scoops right in the nether regions. His eyes bulged, and he started to yell about two octaves higher than normal, "son of …" he cursed and flopped to the ground.

Mrs. Kushinski instantly burst onto the scene. "What happened?" she yelled as she approached and saw the two boys rolling around in the grass.

Scoops was holding his crotch crying out in anguish while Riley clutched his stomach, laughing hysterically. Neither of them could breathe.

"Is everyone alright?" she asked. "And did I hear what I think I did? You better be talking about a female dog!"

The boys quickly sobered up. They both mouthed a silent response to her.

"What?" she demanded. She strained to hear them as if they were a mute acapella band.

Riley finally got the words out. "Seven to six, mom." He gasped for another breath. "Seven to six!"

Mrs. Kushinski looked at both boys skeptically.

Scoops had finally pulled himself to his knees. "Yep, scores seven to six. Riley beat me."

"I hope so," she said as she put her hand on her hips and stormed back into the house.

As Riley and Scoops took a break on the back porch, Riley's mom brought out a jug of cold iced tea and three tall glasses full of ice.

"Thanks, Mrs. Kushinski," Scoops said gratefully, immediately grabbing a glass and placing it between his legs.

Riley looked at the third glass. "Are you joining us, mom?"

"No, but your friend is," she answered, pointing to Emily as she walked out of the patio doors as if she was the surprise guest on a talk show.

Riley jumped up, "Emily, what are you doing here?"

Scoops looked past her as if he was at the arrivals gate, waiting for a long-lost love to return. "Where is Lisa?"

Mrs. Kushinski wiped her hands on her apron and walked back into the house to give them some privacy.

"She is not here," Emily replied woefully.

The boys instantly knew that something wasn't right.

"What's wrong?" Riley asked, his voice laden with concern.

Emily hesitated as if she was just about to flip the release button in a B52 bomber over enemy territory where innocent lives may be in danger.

"Is she alright?" Scoops asked her.

Emily looked at Scoops apologetically. "She can't go out tonight."

The boys' faces dropped. "What?" they chorused.

Emily stopped dipping her toe in the water and jumped right in. "Lisa's dad found out that we went out with you last night and that we had plans to go out again tonight, and he lost his mind."

"Emilio!" Scoops snorted. "Wasn't much mind to lose."

"He won't let her go." She looked at Riley, hoping he would support her rather than reprimand her. "I don't think I can go without her."

Riley gave her an understanding, but disappointed nod.

"Emilio," Scoops repeated numbly, "what a jerk."

"What are you going to do?" Riley asked.

Emily could hardly look at him. "Well, that is the part you are really not going to like."

"Why?" Riley asked, already feeling dejected. "What could be worse?"

"Dr. Fiore is making us go out with him, Lisa's mom," she paused and looked away, "and Todd and Randle."

Riley sighed heavily. "Yeah, that is worse."

After another dismal moment, Emily broke the silence, "I have to go. Lisa's mom's cat is missing."

"What kind of cat?" Riley asked, trying his best to hide his dour mood.

"A tabby cat. Why? Have you seen it?"

"Nope."

"I hate cats," Scoops declared.

Emily looked at Riley and offered a small smile.

Riley reciprocated as she turned slowly and walked back in the house. He didn't show her out.

"I hate cats," Scoops repeated.

Riley was just about to refresh him on his whole love everyone and everything sermon, but just before he did, he noticed a tear was welling up in the corner of one of his eyes.

Scoops must have sensed Riley could tell he was about to cry and bolted to his feet. He sniffled and hocked a big manly loogi in one of Mrs. Kushinski's flowerpots.

"Whatever," he said. "No regrets, we're going out tonight, buddy."

"Yes, we are." Riley concurred as he emptied Emily's glass of ice on the lawn. "Tuxes and all."

17
CRESCENDO

Riley stood downtown, looking at his reflection in the mirror of a large department store window. "We look legit," he told Scoops.

Scoops walked up beside him. His bow tie loose and his untucked shirt hanging out from under his suit coat. "Sure do."

"So, what do you want to do?" Riley asked.

"Let the good times roll," Scoops answered confidently. "I say we just walk around until something good happens."

Riley looked in the window and chuckled to himself. As he turned to fix his hair, he saw a bright red Lamborghini convertible cruise by behind them. It was Emilio and Mrs. Fiore. Lisa and Todd were in the backseat. He quickly turned around and faced his greatest fear. Tailing them was Randle and his old beater of a Buick with Emily in the passenger seat. She looked beautiful as her long curly blonde hair blew softly in the wind. Riley gasped for air and clutched at his chest. His heart ached in a way he would have never understood only two short days before.

Scoops turned around and saw them. "Well, I'll be," he muttered. He looked hopelessly at Riley as if they were outnumbered in a battlefield and could only watch helplessly as the rest of their army retreated. "There they go."

"We have to stop this?" Riley said.

Scoops didn't respond. His downcast eyes told the story. He had lost the will to fight and was waiting submissively for the fatal blow.

Riley slapped him on the shoulder. "Come on, let's go. We have to follow them!"

"Why?" Scoops moaned. "What's the use, Riley?"

Riley grabbed him by the shoulders.

"Pull yourself together, man! They have our girls." Riley did his best William Wallace impression, "they may ruin our shoes, bore us to death, but they will never take our girls!"

Scoops remained dazed and started quoting Winston Churchill. "We shall fight on the beaches. We shall fight—"

"Scoops!" Riley shouted as loud as he could in his face trying snap him out of it. "The girls!" Riley shook him so hard Scoops' teeth chattered.

"Lisa," Scoops softly repeated as if he was waking from a coma. He shook his head to regain his composure. "Let's go get our girls."

The two cars rounded the corner as the boys started their pursuit.

"Slow down!" Scoops yelled as he tried to keep up with Riley. He started taking his shoes off as he ran.

"What are you doing?" Riley shouted back at him.

"Taking off my shoes!"

"Why?"

"I can't keep up."

"They're men's dress shoes, not high heels!" Riley yelled as he raced around the corner with Scoops at least twenty paces behind.

When Scoops finally lumbered up to the corner, Riley tackled him to the ground and pulled him behind a parked car.

"Get down!" Riley shouted as if they were about to be hit by a mortar.

Scoops legs were Jell-O, and he collided hard into the vehicle setting off an ear-splitting car alarm.

"Geez," Riley said looking at Scoops in disbelief. He couldn't tell what was louder, the car alarm or Scoops' wheezing.

Every bystander on the street was staring at them as if they just witnessed a fatal accident.

"They are going to see us," Riley said anxiously. He looked around and spotted a nearby barbershop with the door propped open by a Harley kickstand. Riley dragged Scoops inside like a wounded soldier.

The Barber

Cut hair matted the tile floor. The air was musty and smelled like body odor with a hint of stale aftershave.

"Eww," Scoops said he brushed strands of hair from his socks. "Is that dandruff?"

"Well, put your shoes back on," Riley ordered.

A very deep voice rumbled from a dark corner of the room. "Can I help you?"

The boys looked, but all they could see was the red flicker of a burning cigarette. A massive werewolf of a man emerged from the darkness. The cigarette lit up brightening the room as he inhaled enough smoke to evacuate a small village. As he crept out of the shadows, the boys could make out a red bandana on his head and a beard that was about ten inches long. His arms were like oil barrels, and his legs were like redwood tree trunks. The mirrors on the wall shook with every tile-splitting step he took. He had a morbid tattoo of a massive snake eating a smaller snake on his left arm that started from his wrists and wrapped all the way up to his shoulders until it disappeared under a black leather biker vest.

Horrified, the boys' eyes locked.

Riley gulped. "No, we're fine, no thanks."

"Yep we're all good," Scoops concurred, his voice quivering.

The stout man scratched his chin under his long beard, cracked his knuckles, and crossed his arms slowly. "Then do you mind telling me why you are in my shop?"

"Hiding, sir," Riley responded.

"Hiding," the man replied. "Usually, people don't hide where I can find them."

"No doubt, sir." Scoops said looking at Riley big-eyed and then back at the giant. "You are a scary man."

"Excuse me?" The man stepped forward with a thud.

"I mean you are very large, intimidating, a little frightening…"

While Scoops had the man's attention and continued digging

himself a deeper hole, Riley took the opportunity to look out the window and relocate Emily.

"They are going in the theatre!" Riley yelled.

Emily looked gorgeous. She wore a strapless red evening dress that hugged and highlighted every curve of her body with sequin embellishments.

"Who is going into the theatre?" the man asked, his neck creaking as he turned to look at Riley.

"Our girlfriends," Scoop answered bravely as if having a girlfriend made him a real tough guy.

"Girlfriends? You mean those two fine looking ladies going into the theatre with those other two guys?" He pointed over their heads, and the boys went cross-eyed, staring at his gigantic finger.

"Yeah," Scoops answered, still trying to use his big boy voice and intimidate his adversary.

At this point, Riley's only threat came from Randle. He could care less about the monstrosity that towered over him.

"They don't look like your girlfriends." A large grin started to crevice the big barber's burly beard as he started into a laugh. He sounded like a Freightliner trying to turnover in the middle of a snowstorm.

"Well, they aren't really," Riley admitted. "Almost."

"They will be," Scoops said confidently. The laugh had exposed a softer side of the man Scoops felt he could exploit.

"I like your tattoos, sir," Scoops complimented as he observed the man's ink. They completely covered his right arm and neck. "They must have taken a very long time?"

"What's that supposed to mean?" he growled. "Because I'm fat?"

Scoops flinched. Again, he started backpedaling. "No, of course not, I mean all that detail."

The big man put his hands on his hips and started his slow rumble of a laugh again.

Scoops smiled awkwardly, still not getting a good read on the mammoth and unsure what way the whole situation was going to turn. Was this guy that sensitive or was he high on Barbicide. "Mind if I ask what the snake eating another snake symbolizes?"

Riley shot him a dirty look, warning him to tread lightly.

The man looked down at his left arm. "There is always a bigger snake," he replied, prophesizing as if he was Confucius.

"I don't get it," Scoops confessed.

Riley shot him another death glare.

"If you choose to be a snake, you have to remember there is always going to be a bigger snake that will eat you." He flicked his cigarette butt on the floor as he preached. The smell of burnt hair immediately invaded their nostrils.

Riley pretended to scratch his upper lip so he could take a deep sniff of his hand and mask the smell.

"Ingenious," Scoops said inquisitively. He shrugged his shoulders at Riley to indicate he had no idea what was going on. "I never thought of that, very deep, sir." He nodded along as if he understood completely and couldn't agree more. "And that one?" he added, pointing at a tattoo of a knife through a skull. "What's that supposed to mean?"

The man pulled his beard aside and looked at his other arm. That is just a knife in a skull," he said. It needed no further explanation.

"Charming," Riley remarked as he grabbed Scoops by the shoulder to shuffle out the entrance and back outside to the street.

"Wait a minute!" the beast of a man barked.

"Yes?" they responded, clenching their teeth, both scared stiff.

"You guys need tickets?"

"Tickets?" Riley repeated.

"Yeah," the big man scratched his beard, "tickets to watch the Orchestra?"

"Orchestra," the boys repeated in unison as if all the pieces were starting to fit together.

"That is where they are going," Riley said, staring out the window at the theatre. "What an elegant and equally incredibly boring choice, Randle and Todd."

"Yeah," Scoops cackled awkwardly. "What was there no tickets left for the Symphony?"

Riley stared blankly back at Scoops. "Same thing you idiot."

"Do you need tickets?" the man asked again impatiently as if he had a room full of waiting customers.

"Yes, yes! We do," Riley instantly replied.

The man thumped his way to the counter. He opened a small box next to the cash register that looked like it might hold a revolver and reached inside.

The boys began to squirm.

He reached in and grabbed two tickets. "A customer gave me these," he said as he looked closely at the stubs to make sure they were the correct ones. "Orchestra is not really my thing."

"You don't say," Scoops heckled the man that looked more like a Sasquatch than he did a barber. "I wouldn't guess cutting hair was either."

Riley shot him another cautionary glare.

"Thank you so much, sir," Riley said quickly, not letting the big man dwell on Scoops' comment. He reached out to shake the man's hand.

The man looked at him surprised, then reciprocated, his hand swallowing Riley's.

"The name's Bashful," he said.

The boys just stared at each other. This guy was full of surprises.

"Nice to meet you, sir, thanks for the tickets."

Just in case one day he would recall the favor, the boys didn't offer their names.

As soon as Riley had safely stowed the tickets in his suit pocket, they ran for freedom before either of them were tempted to say another word.

The Line-Up

"Tickets please?" The man in the red hat demanded as they approached the entrance to the theatre. The name etched into his vest read Bill.

Riley tapped Scoops on his shoulder as if he were Scoops' mother. "Tuck in your shirt."

"Tickets?" Bill called out again, his voice grittier than coarse sandpaper. He stuck his left hand out at Riley. With his right hand, he raised a cigarette to his lips.

Riley gave him the two tickets then coughed as he inhaled a cloud of second-hand smoke.

Bill eyed their tickets, holding his cigarette loosely between his lips and ripped them in two. He handed the two halves back to Riley.

Scoops was eyeing the name on his shirt as if they were about to commence into an engaging dialogue. "You prefer Bill or William, sir?"

"If you leave, you need a stamp," he grumbled, his cigarette bouncing up and down in his mouth blowing ashes down the lineup of people that followed. "Bill," he said, slowly tapping the name on his shirt with a stained yellow finger. He desperately needed to clean under his fingernail which was packed with either dirt or scratch ticket filings.

"Stamp to get out and a gas mask to get in, hey Bill?" Scoops said chuckling, nudging a random symphony enthusiast beside him.

The gatekeeper, Bill, not William, looked at Riley unamused and gestured at Scoops, "he with you?"

"Yep, see you later," Riley answered quickly grabbing Scoops and dragging him inside the lobby before Bill decided he had other plans for them.

"Wait!" Scoops cried as the door closed behind them. "We should ask Bill if he knows Rhonda over at Bridgeport Fun Park."

Coat Check

Safely inside the lobby, the boys found their way to a coat check room where not a single guest seemed to be checking anything. There were no attendants in sight, and the boys walked right in.

"I don't think anyone else here is wearing a tux, Riley." Scoops said and looked around the lobby. "We look like were in the band."

Riley nodded but wasn't listening. He was on a mission to find Emily. He scanned the crowd and instantly froze. It was Principal Wentworth.

"What is it?" Scoops asked.

"Principal Wentworth," Riley whispered.

"Let's go say hi," Scoops said as if he was excited to see him. Riley grabbed him by his suit coat as he started to walk towards him.

As Riley and Scoops argued about whether or not they should say hi, a tall, thin man with a bushy mustache and an attractive redhead came up to the counter.

"Please check," the man directed as he handed over a long brown double-breasted trench coat.

The man's voice was familiar. The boys looked at each other confused and turned to examine the lady on his arm. She was dressed years above her age and was clearly wearing too much makeup.

Her features reminded Riley of Miss Carpenter, but he shrugged it off, grabbed the lookalike Inspector Gadget coat and immediately delegated the task to Scoops.

The man stared at Riley, then at Scoops, back to Riley. His eyebrows began to rise to the ceiling.

It was Mr. Tillweed!

"Mr. Dill Weed!" Scoops announced pleasantly. "How great to see you."

"Tillweed!" he shot back. His lip quivering, loosening a poorly glued on mustache.

"And who is this young lady?" Scoops asked. "Does Miss Carpenter know?"

The woman's face flushed red, and she unlocked her arm from Mr. Tillweed's.

The boys leaned forward over the counter, examining her out as if she were a rare fish swimming in an aquarium.

"Oooh," they both said nodding. "It is Miss Carpenter."

"Hi boys," she said shame-faced.

The boys carried on as if it was no big deal.

"Didn't know this was a costume party, sir?" Riley said as Scoops went through the pockets of Mr. Tillweed's coat.

"What on earth are you doing, Floyd?" Mr. Tillweed demanded.

Scoops lifted the collar of Mr. Tillweed's coat and folded it back neatly in place. He handed the coat back to Mr. Tillweed. "Just checking your coat, it looks good."

Mr. Tillweed snatched the coat out of his hands and snarled. "Keep your mouth shut."

"You guys keep your mouth shut," Scoops shot back.

"Yeah no more of that kissing and stuff," Riley added. "Even though everybody already knows about you."

Mr. Tillweed looked around the lobby as if he was scouting for Principal Wentworth. He patted his mustache with the tips of his fingers to reposition it.

"Oh," Riley picked up on the clue. "Except Principal Wentworth." He pointed his thumb at Scoops. "I imagine he hasn't heard about his glass-shattering discus performance quite yet?"

"No," Tillweed replied. "And we plan on telling the Principal on Monday."

"You're going to spill the beans?" Riley jabbed as if that was impossible. "You sure he won't hear it from anyone else?"

"Yes," Miss Carpenter emphasized as if her input would keep the boys and the rest of the school quiet for another day. "We didn't want to distract him from his big performance tonight."

Mr. Tillweed cleared his throat. "Out of respect."

Riley looked at Scoops and then back at the sneaky teachers. "Hence the getup?" he said, pointing at their ridiculous outfits.

"Yes," Mr. Tillweed nodded.

"Good thinking," Scoops said, emphasizing how insane it all was.

"Good luck with that," Riley added.

Scoops spoke up. "Miss Carpenter."

"Yes, Jack?" she answered.

He passed her a tissue and rubbed his nose, "just in case."

She turned red again, but this time, it wasn't from embarrassment. She threw the tissue back at Scoops and stormed off angrily.

Mr. Tillweed just stood speechless, shaking his head at Scoops.

Scoops nudged Riley. "Hey look, it's that old gal from the office." He pointed at Ms. Fitzpatrick. "Everybody is here."

"Oh yeah, it is her. Ms. Fitz!" Riley called across the room.

She turned and greeted them with a big smile.

"Look, Mr...." Riley turned back to Mr. Tillweed, but he had already darted off.

Ms. Fitz approached them. She still had her bifocals on, butterfly brooch, and her old red cardigan. In fact, nothing about her wardrobe was any different.

"Well, hello," she said cheerfully. "You are just the boys I wanted to see." She held up a tabby cat. "Look, I found Mr. Wiggles!"

Riley gulped. "Great news!" he said, staring wide-eyed at the cat.

"What map did you find him on?" Scoops asked curiously. "Was it a big X or small x?"

"He just came home?"

"Home?" Riley asked.

"Well, yes," she explained, "I was just out at the grocery store, and saw he had crawled into someone's convertible. It was a good thing I got to him just in time. He would have overheated in there."

"Yeah, good thing," Scoops agreed.

"In the convertible?" Riley said frowning at Scoops. "That means it has no top, you know."

Scoops looked at him as if he was stupid. "I know what convertible means, I am a huge fan of convertible girls." He laughed and offered a high five to Ms. Fitzpatrick who stared vacantly back at him.

Riley shook his head and looked back at Mr. Fitz.

"How exactly is that home?"

"I don't live at the grocery store," she explained.

"I know Ms. Fitz. You said Mr. Wiggles came home."

She listened intently to Riley nodding in complete agreement.

Riley continued to interrogate her. "But you just told us you found him at the store."

"Yes," she replied.

The boys waited for Ms. Fitzpatrick to finish, but apparently, that was all.

Scoops tried to fill in the blanks. "Then you brought it home?"

"Yes," she said. "Then, Mr. Wiggles came home." She lifted Mr. Wiggles to her lips and gave him a big kiss between the ears.

Riley gave up, "How did you get him in here?"

"The man at the front said I could bring him in."

"Bill?" Riley asked.

"No, he was free," she responded.

Riley emitted a hopeless sigh and moved on. "What about allergies, dander, etc.?"

Scoops looked at Riley as if none of it was a big deal. "Remember Bill, Riley?" he asked, raising his fingers to his mouth, pretending he was smoking, "not sure old Bill cares much about what goes into people's lungs."

An announcement played through the lobby.

Good evening Ladies and Gentlemen, the performance will be starting in ten minutes. Please finish your refreshments and make your way to your seats. Ushers are standing by to help direct all guests.

"Oh, dear," Ms. Fitz said. "We'd better make our way to our seat, Mr. Wiggles." She turned to leave, "it was great to see you."

"Nice lady," Scoops said as they watched her funnel into the theatre with the rest of the crowd. Behind her, a woman sneezed.

"She is out of her mind," Riley said to Scoops.

"Why do you think that?"

Riley turned and stared at him in disbelief. He shouted at him as quiet as possible. "That was Lisa's mom's cat!"

"Oh," Scoops said, "I thought it was Mr. Wiggles."

Riley shook his head. "There is no Mr. Wiggles! How the heck did you get good grades, Scoops?"

Riley saw Lisa and Emily and ducked back into the coat check. "There they are! They're are going into the lower level with Randle and Todd."

"Of course they are," Scoops blurted.

Riley exhaled deeply. "Look at them. They look great."

Scoops turned and eyed his friend.

Riley continued, "Emily looks amazing."

Scoops looked relieved. "Good, I was worried you were talking about Randle and Todd."

"Why would I be talking about Randle and Todd?" Riley snorted.

Scoops answered, "I don't know, that's why I was worried. We have to get closer to them."

Out of thin air, Hans from the tuxedo rental shop appeared in the crowd and walked up to Dr. Fiore.

Scoops gasped and started to panic. "It's, it's, it's Hans," he stuttered, "and he is talking to the psychic."

"Psychiatrist," Riley corrected him.

"I told you he was a psycho serial killer."

"That doesn't prove anything," Riley argued.

"Yes it does, he must be a patient." Scoops stared down at his and Riley's tuxedos. "I can't believe we are wearing dead men's suits."

Just then, there was a booming voice from behind them. "Can I help you, gentlemen?"

The Usher

They turned to see the shortest usher they had ever seen. He scowled up at them with his tiny arms on his hips.

Scoops put his hand on Riley's chest as if to let him know he had everything under control. "No, sir," he answered and nodded at Riley.

"Can I see your tickets, please?" the little man demanded.

Riley looked at Scoops as if he was waiting for him to finish his glorious plan. Scoops just stared back blankly at him. The plan had reached its conclusion. There were no appendices.

Riley knew they had to get the girls and couldn't give their seat location away to the usher. Thankfully, he was quick on his feet, "we are with the band, sir."

The small man looked at them from head to toe, analyzing their tuxes.

This could work, Riley thought.

"Then why are you back here?" he asked.

He was buying it.

Scoops came back to life, "Rhonda, sir."

"Rhonda?" both Riley and the small man asked.

"Yes. Rhonda, sir," Scoops pointed to Rhonda from Bridgeport Fun Park. She was flustered as usual and rushing to get through the crowd of people. She wore the exact same tuxedo as the boys only twice the material.

"What about Rhonda?" the man asked.

It worked. Riley and Scoops really did look like they were in the band!

"She asked us to get something for her," Scoops answered.

"What?" the angry little usher asked.

"I don't think we have time sir," Scoops said, pointing to the overhead speakers. "The announcer said the show is going to start very soon."

The man could care less.

"Cigarettes, sir," Riley chimed in. "She wanted us to grab her some cigarettes."

Riley was onto something. "Yep cigarettes, sir," Scoops tagged back in. "She told us to ask Bill for some."

"Bill?" the tiny man snarled.

"Yep, Bill."

"Then why are you in here?" he asked gesturing to the empty coat check.

"We thought we would check her coat first, sir."

The man turned around and surveyed the room. "No one wears a coat on an evening like this."

"Hate to argue with you," Scoops said. "But one guy did. He's kind of a special one though."

The announcement came on again.

Good evening again Ladies and Gentlemen, the performance will be starting in five minutes. If you haven't made it to your seats, please continue to make your way into the auditorium. Ushers are standing by to help direct all guests.

"Some might be kneeling," Scoops whispered to Riley as he nodded at the tiny usher.

"What was that?" the tiny usher barked.

"He just said we better go," Riley quickly answered. "We are on soon."

"Yeah, Rhonda is going to wonder where we are," Scoops added. "She really needed a smoke."

"Ok, well you tell her when you see her Cliff is not happy."

"Who is Cliff?" Scoops asked. "Don't you mean Bill?"

"I am Cliff!" he shouted at Scoops. "Her husband!"

"Oh," Scoops said. "Well, who's Bill?"

"The ticket guy," Riley reminded him.

"Oh yeah."

"No," the angry usher Cliff muttered, "Bill is the clown who keeps feeding my Rhonda cigarettes like she is Big Bertha. I am starting to think something is going on."

"Big Bertha, sir?" Scoops asked not getting the reference.

"I love that game," Riley said. "You play, sir?"

"I dabble," he responded as if they were talking about polo or tennis. "Come on, I can clear a path to help you get backstage."

Riley had won him over with their shared love for Feeding Big Bertha.

"Commonality breeds camaraderie," Riley said to Scoops as they followed the tiny man through the crowd.

"Nice," Scoops said, "you should get that tattooed on you like Bashful."

Backstage

The door clicked closed behind them, and the boys looked at each other stunned. Somehow, they had made it backstage. All around them musicians in tuxes nervously tuned and fiddled with their instruments. The boys blended right in.

"No wonder these are the most popular rental," Riley said to Scoops pulling on his lapel. "They must have all been rented from Hans."

"They do look pretty sharp," Scoops replied. "Wouldn't want to be buried in anything less."

What sounded like a child's voice startled them. "You guys sure are cutting it close."

"What close?" Scoops asked suspiciously eyeing up a mysterious figure in the dark.

"I thought I could just sit back and enjoy the show."

"Who are you?" Scoops asked, squinting into the darkness.

"Flynn," the figure said as if they should have already known. A young child stepped into the light. "You the fill-ins?" he asked.

"For what?"

"Late and funny, double threat, eh?" the chatty kid smirked. "I like your style." He paused thoughtfully. "Unless you aren't actually in the band, then I will have to call security."

Riley had inched his way to the curtain and was looking out over the audience. He scanned the murmuring crowd for Emily. When he finally found her, he saw Randle put his arm around her and his heart sank. Then something wonderful happened. Emily put her hand behind her neck and flicked her hair in Randle's face. Randle blinked but didn't move. She flicked her hair again. Randle didn't take the hint, he just sat sniffing as if he were face deep in a lilac bush.

Riley had to save her. "Yes, we are the fill-ins," he declared.

The little kid looked at him relieved, "jeepers guys, this job is stressful enough, alright. You don't need to tease me."

Scoops rolled his eyes at Riley and whispered, "musicians, man they are sensitive."

The kid's ears shot up. "I heard that!"

Riley tapped him lightly on the shoulder to smooth things over. "Don't worry kid. We are musicians too."

"Well," the kid sighed. "I am not really a musician yet. I'm working on it."

"Then what do you do?" Scoops interest was piqued.

"Help backstage," he said as his eyes lit up. "I get the musician's instruments ready, help set up the stage and things like that."

"So…you are like a roadie," Riley pointed out.

"Yeah, I guess so," he said proudly, "an orchestra roadie."

"Careful son," Scoops warned as if we were a young king's chief advisor. "That can be a dark path to follow."

Scoops took his turn peering out behind the curtain. He scanned the audience looking for Lisa and found her nestled in between Dr. Fiore and Todd. Next to Emilio was Lisa's mom. She looked distraught, her eyes puffy like she hadn't been able to stop crying all day. If she only knew her cat was only four rows back, nestled cozily in the moth-eaten dress of Ms. Fitzpatrick.

Mr. Tillweed and Miss Carpenter sat directly behind Ms. Fitzpatrick. The librarian was hard to miss with her bright red hair and the fact that she seemed to be sneezing every thirty seconds.

Lisa looked like a Paris runway model. Her long black hair flowed freely over her shoulders. She wore a short black cocktail dress with lace covering her shoulders and deep v-neckline. The floral pattern barely exposed a hint of her soft skin. She looked breathtaking but incredibly bored. Scoops gawked at her as she sat, staring down into her lap.

"On her phone, as always," he whispered to himself.

Lisa lifted her hand from her lap and studied it.

"It's not her phone," Scoops said, his face brightening. "It's my ring!"

"What are you rambling on about?" Riley asked.

Scoops ignored him. "Riley, are you thinking what I am thinking?"

"Nope, I am thinking we go on stage and bring down the house for our girls."

Scoops looked surprised. "That is what I was thinking."

Flynn looked at them as if they had forgotten one major detail. "You are going to need an instrument. So, what do you two play?"

"Flute," Scoops blurted.

Riley started laughing until he saw Scoops nodding his head towards him. Scoops finished, "he plays the flute."

"Wait…" Riley tried to interject, but it was too late.

"Great, that's what they told me you played." Flynn handed Riley a long narrow case. "Should be ready, but check it over, you know how us musicians are." He winked at Riley. "And you are on percussion, right?" he asked Scoops.

"Percussion, what's that?" Scoops asked, "I think I prefer oboe."

The kid looked at him in disbelief, "you prefer oboe over drums?" Flynn held a pair of drumsticks up. "We needed percussion."

Scoops snatched the sticks as fast as he could. "Nope, drums, definitely drums for me."

Flynn looked back at Riley. "I admire you, man."

"Oh yeah, why's that?" Scoops asked before Riley could.

"To be able just to jump in last minute and cover Beverly's solo. She has been working on that for months."

"Beverly's what?" Riley gasped as he stared down at the mysterious silver instrument he had just taken out of the case.

"Solo," Scoops repeated coolly as if he understood what it meant.

"I didn't know you played." A raspy voice caught them off guard. The smell of smoke should have warned them, but they missed it. They turned to stand face to face with Rhonda.

"A little," Riley said, preparing for the worst.

"They are just modest," the kid chimed in. "These are the fill-ins from out of town."

"Uh-huh," she said suspiciously. "I bet."

Riley and Scoops stared at a gigantic tuba in Rhonda's hands trying to decide what was larger, Rhonda or the brass instrument.

"Nice tuba," Scoops offered politely.

Behind them, Principal Wentworth bellowed, "alright everyone, we are on in thirty seconds, everybody quickly to their seats!"

"Great," Riley choked to Scoops. "He is going to recognize us for sure."

"What is that thing on his head?" Scoops asked, pointing with a drumstick to a mat of long curly black hair on Mr. Wentworth.

"Looks like a wig," Riley chuckled.

"You guys have never worked with the conductor?" Flynn asked suspiciously.

"Doesn't matter, we have a show to do," Scoops replied coolly, pushing him aside as he twirled his drumsticks in his fingers like a rock star.

The Performance

Riley pretended to clean his flute while he waited for all the other musicians to take their seats. Once they were all sitting, he saw an empty chair next to three other flutists directly in front of Principal Wentworth.

Riley turned to Flynn and pointed to a group of musicians in the back with French horns, "I think I will just sit back here with these people."

That was obviously not an option. "Those are the brasses, you are with the woodwinds," the kid pointed to the empty chair.

Riley scoffed, "brasses, of course, always do whatever they want." He shook his head and lectured. "Don't let the man get you down, kid." Riley started to make his way to his seat.

As he got close, he watched Wentworth pick lint off his suit coat with his left hand. In his right hand, he held his shiny baton. He kept clearing his throat as if he was going to start singing. His suit was wide open because there was no possible way he could do up the buttons over his belly and the tails on his tuxedo were wrinkled as if they had been used all day as a seat cushion. He was already sweating, and his ghastly wig was not helping keep him cool.

Riley squeezed his way through the violins and took his seat. "Hi woodwinds," he said cheerfully. "What are we playing?"

They stared at him astonished. No one responded.

He looked at his music stand and started flipping through the pages.

The shuffling of the pages was enough to catch Wentworth's attention. He saw Riley, and his face went ghostly white. "Kushinski!" he snarled. "What are you doing here?"

Riley settled into his chair as if he were an angel sent from heaven to save the evening. "Hi, Principal Wentworth," he responded calmly, "I can't read this." He pointed to the sheet music. "You don't happen to have tabs, do you?"

"Tablature!" Wentworth shouted back.

"Yeah, you know, numbers instead of dots, I have no idea what this means."

Wentworth ignored him. "How did you get in here?" he demanded.

Riley turned, pointing to the far back corner where Rhonda was sitting already looking exhausted from propping up her tuba. "Her."

Wentworth shot her a death glare, and she immediately started shaking her head from side to side.

A raucous commenced in the percussion section.

Wentworth turned to his left where Scoops had begun fighting with another percussionist. "I want to play these big drums," Scoops shouted at an old man whose pants were barely staying on his hips. The man was petrified. He grasped his mallets in his hands as if they were an IV pole.

"You are on cymbals and triangle," he told Scoops with a British accent. He pointed to the last available spot on the edge of the stage.

Scoops tried to reach for the mallet. "No way, you play those."

"No, I play the timpani," he wailed. "I am the timpanist."

"Timpani," Scoops laughed. "Those are drums."

By now, the full orchestra focused on Scoops.

"Are you kidding right now?" The man was starting to tremble but doing his best to act brave. He looked at Scoops as if he had just caught him in the middle of the night trashing his home. "A timpani is kettledrums."

"That would make it timpanis!" Scoop shouted and started to walk away. "Timpani," he scoffed. "Sounds lame anyway." When he finally made it to where he was supposed to be, he picked up a triangle and wand. He looked an attractive and much older violinist and stated as if he were justifying a poor career choice, "it takes a real man to play this you know, anyone can hit a drum."

Wentworth's wig was already sliding down as sweat beaded off his forehead. "You two—" he started to say, but it was too late. The house lights went dim. The murmuring crowd went silent, and the only sound was the whir of the big red curtain's motor.

The announcer came on.

Ladies and Gentlemen, Bridgeport Symphony Orchestra, presents, "A Night at the Movies." Please remain seated, turn all personal handheld devices off, and remain quiet until after the performance. Most importantly, please enjoy yourself.

In the crowd, Emily turned to Randle who still had his arm around her, "yeah be quiet, people are trying to sleep."

Lisa heard her and hit her on the thigh.

"What is he doing here?" Todd blurted out as the curtains opened.

Scoops was standing in the left corner of the stage, scanning the crowd with his hand over his eyes as if he was an explorer scouting for land.

Dr. Fiore was on the edge of his seat, waiting for the concert to begin. When he saw Scoops, his eyes widened. He sat back and ran his forefinger and thumb through his dark goatee. "Hmm," he whispered to Lisa's mom. "I wasn't aware he played."

"Who?" she asked, still wiping away tears from the corners of her puffy eyes.

Scoops finally spotted them in the dark auditorium and gave them a big wave.

Todd watched in horror as Dr. Fiore stopped rubbing his goatee, raised his arm, and gave Scoops a thumbs-up. He then leaned forward, turning to look down the aisle at Lisa.

Todd was going head-to-head with Wentworth for the title of the reddest face in the auditorium.

From out of the silence behind them, Miss Carpenter let out a window-shattering sneeze. Everyone in the auditorium jumped in their seats.

Riley, unfazed was still flipping through the sheet music. "I know this one," he said to the stuffy woman beside him. "Good movie."

After weighing his options and realizing they were minimal, Wentworth raised his arms in the air. The musicians immediately followed, raising their instruments as if strings tied them to Mr. Wentworth's baton.

Riley began raising his flute to his lips as if he was about to play the clarinet.

Wentworth stared at him in horror.

Riley felt six hundred plus eyes burning into him and looked to his left, noticing the error of his ways. He flipped the flute from ninety degrees to forty-five degrees. "Just kidding," he mouthed.

An old lady giggled in the front row. "I hadn't seen that before," she whispered to her husband who didn't seem to appreciate the humor as much as she did.

"It's Riley," Emily breathed.

Randle saw Riley and removed his arm from behind her and sat forward as if he was going to leapfrog over ten rows onto the stage and pummel him.

Wentworth raised his arms an extra inch to reset and ready the musicians.

Scoops had finally discovered there was music on the stand in front of him. "What song are we on?" he asked the snare drummer beside him.

The man ignored him.

Wentworth took a deep breath that caused the other thirty-plus musicians to follow suit as if they were trying to suck up all the oxygen in the room. The violinist and cellists raised their bows. The woodwinds licked their lips while the brasses puckered theirs.

Suddenly, chimes rang out through the auditorium startling everyone except Scoops who had walked over to a set of chimes next to the timpani. He glared at the old man as if he had died and therefore severely dropped the ball.

Scoops slowly returned to his place on stage right then he turned to the old lady in the front. "When you hear the sound of the chimes, you will know it is time to turn the page."

The lady stared back stone-faced but then cracked a small awkward smile.

"Let's begin, sir," Scoops instructed Principal Wentworth from the back of the Orchestra.

Wentworth didn't respond. He stood frozen on his platform, dripping sweat like a water fountain.

Riley tried to blow in his flute. "Phhh," he tried again, "phhh." He turned to the lady beside him, who was doing her best to ignore him. "I think mine is broken."

Wentworth couldn't raise his hand in the air any higher, so he got the band's attention by standing on his tiptoes.

Riley took the opportunity to check out his shoes. They matched. Good job, sir, he thought. Behind Wentworth, he caught a glimpse of Emily staring back at him.

"What are you doing?" she mouthed.

Riley shrugged.

At once, Wentworth dropped his arms, and the musicians burst into a song from Gladiator.

Riley just stared at Emily.

"Play," she mouthed.

Riley shook his head as if that wasn't an option and began to look around him. It is quite beautiful, he thought. He turned to Principal Wentworth who seemed to have settled down a bit. The performance, minus a couple of setbacks, seemed to be off to a relatively good start. He waved his hands in the air emphatically, the shiny baton in his right hand flailing everywhere. Riley had no idea what any of it meant, and no one else seemed to be looking at the big man. Over his left shoulder, he turned to look back at Rhonda. Her face was beet red, but somehow, she was still blowing away on her tuba. He turned to his right and watched Scoops through a swarm of violinist's elbows and bows. It looked like Scoops was actually trying. He reminded Riley of Todd, bobbing up and down preparing for a high jump attempt but instead of running, he was banging the triangle on every fourth bob. Scoops effort inspired him, and he placed the flute to his lips.

Wentworth instantly caught sight of him and shot him a death glare.

Riley slowly lowered the flute again and decided to just look at Emily. When he saw her across the large room, she was still staring back at him. He couldn't just sit up there and do nothing.

He raised the flute to his lips again.

Wentworth gritted his teeth to brace himself, shaking his head so frantically that his wig juked from side to side.

Riley placed his fingers on the keys and blew into the flute.

To the conductor's relief, it still didn't make a sound.

Riley pretended to play as he stared deep into Emily's eyes. She had an incredibly impressed look on her face and must have thought he was such a quick learner, a real natural.

While Emily watched in amazement, Randle sat scowling at Riley. He was not as fascinated by Riley's hidden talents.

Randle and Todd had had enough. They simultaneously leaned forward and looked at each other. Randle nodded his head, indicating to Todd that it was time to take matters into their own hands. Todd sprang into action and started to shuffle down the aisle, over Lisa, towards Randle. "No," he whispered, "the other way."

"What?" Todd asked Randle, clueless that he sat only three seats in from the aisle.

Randle pointed and waved his open hand, indicating to go in the other direction.

"Oh," he said sheepishly.

The mishap had already created enough of a commotion to draw the ire of other audience members.

Ms. Fitzpatrick shushed them as she stroked the not so Mr. Wiggles. More of the crowd joined in, and the chorus of shushes attracted the attention of the ushers.

Randle crawled over Emily before she had a chance to move her knees to the side, stepping on her open-toed shoes.

"Ouch!" she shouted.

Hearing someone in distress, Rhonda's little usher husband Cliff picked up the pace and caught Todd just as he was squeezing past Dr. and Mrs. Fiore.

"Sit down," he ordered.

The noise from the dark startled Todd, and he sat down immediately, directly on top of Mrs. Fiore.

"Get off!" she screeched, trying to push Todd off her lap.

Dr. Fiore was too into the music to notice. His head tilted back, eyes closed, ears wide open as if he was trying to check the tuning of each instrument.

Randle kept coming. He grabbed Todd and pulled him back off Mrs. Fiore, helping him to his feet.

"Back to your seats!" Cliff ordered again, this time much louder than a whisper.

From behind them, Miss Carpenter let another demon exercising sneeze that shook the acoustic foam that lined the walls and ceiling of the auditorium.

Cliff ducked and covered as if his gunner shelter was under attack.

Todd and Randle used the distraction to make a beeline for the exit.

Miss Carpenter's latest sneeze caused Mr. Wentworth to lose his grip on his baton and drop it on the stage. He frantically looked for it as he continued to wave his hands, trying to keep time. No one noticed except Riley, who was the only one not looking at his sheet music. Riley found the glistening baton resting near his feet and quickly picked it up and passed it to him. Wentworth, for almost a split second, appeared grateful he was there.

The song ended. The audience, to Wentworth's surprise, applauded.

He turned to face the crowd, his wig following him half of the way. He took a deep breath to ensure his voice would carry to the back of the room.

"Ladies and gentlemen, thank you for coming." He looked around slowly as he remembered to pace his words.

"This evening we are sharing with you some of our favourite songs from some of the most popular movies of all time. You may have recognized the last song from the movie Gladiator starring Russel Crowe. He broke into his best Maximus impression. "Are you not entertained?" he shouted at the audience.

No one responded.

Emily had slid over a seat to sit next to Lisa. She held her fist out in front of her, and turned her thumb down as if to condemn the performance to death.

Lisa swatted her arm down quickly before her parents saw.

Wentworth continued, "Our next song you may recognize from the popular movie franchise Star Wars, as written and composed by John Williams." He expected a warm round of applause but instead noticed that the entire audience was no longer paying attention to him.

Like a tightrope walker, Scoops had squeezed his way between the edge of the stage and the violinists. He held the triangle up in the air.

"Hey sir!" he said as he neared the Principal. "This song really calls for some heavy cymbals. I think you should play this." He passed the big man the tiny instrument. "You're not really doing anything with your left hand anyway. Here," he demonstrated, "just hit it with that wand thing in your right hand like this."

Wentworth stared back at him speechless.

The lady in the front giggled again. This time more of the audience joined her. They were starting to believe that Riley and Scoops were an act!

Scoops quickly returned to his place, making sure he said hi to every violinist as he passed them. Nobody responded. They all just stared back at him in disbelief.

When Scoops had returned to his spot, Principal Wentworth raised his arms into the air. As he did, he noticed he was still holding the triangle and immediately dropped it to the floor.

Riley went to pick it up, and Wentworth quickly waved his hand to stop him.

Principal Wentworth raised his arms, softly counted the orchestra in, and they burst into the familiar Star Wars intro.

Scoops started slamming his mallet against the cymbal as if he was knocking the dust out of a wet rug. Crashing cymbals filled the entire hall.

Ms. Fitzpatrick squealed as the not, so Mr. Wiggles jumped from her lap and ran for safety.

The Imperial March sounded more like the Imperial Stampede as every musician did their best to play louder and match the volume of Scoops' cymbals.

Scoops biggest fan in the front row's jaw dropped, and the giddy old lady had to struggle to keep her dentures from rattling out of her gaping mouth.

Even Dr. Fiore had to open his eyes to figure out what was happening.

Wentworth had finally noticed that no one in the orchestra was looking at him and he turned his complete attention on Scoops, gesturing to him to stop by slashing his own throat with his baton.

Scoops was giving it 110% and had broken into a serious sweat. As he wiped his brow with the sleeve of his tux, he caught sight of Wentworth. He looked at the other two percussionists as if the conductor was signaling to them. He pointed to himself and mouthed "me?"

"Yes!" Wentworth yelled back. No one could hear him anyway.

Scoops immediately stopped as if he was dying for a break.

As the orchestra managed to pull the song together, Todd and Randle burst through the unsupervised backstage door.

"Who are you?" Flynn demanded from his dark lair. His voice startling them just as it had scared Riley and Scoops only moments before.

"I'm Todd," Todd announced as if the boy should have expected him.

By now Flynn was pretty certain Riley and Scoops were not who they claimed to be.

"You guys must be the real fill-ins, huh?" he asked. "Man you guys are late."

Todd and Randle looked at each other.

"Yep," Randle said.

"You guys don't look like musicians."

"You don't look like security," Randle shot back.

"I'm not," he bragged. "I'm a roadie."

"Roadie?" Todd repeated. "Orchestras have roadies?"

Back on stage, to no one's displeasure, the Imperial March had ended and Principal Wentworth was trying to gather himself. He fidgeted with his wig, which looked like it was trying to crawl off his bald scalp. He coughed to clear his throat.

The audience was deafly quiet, wincing as if at any moment Scoops was going to strike another cymbal.

"Thank you," Mr. Wentworth bellowed to the crowd.

No one had clapped.

"This next piece you may recognize from the blockbuster Titanic, composed by James Horner." He turned back to the orchestra and raised his arms into the air. By now, his sweat had made it through his undershirt, dress shirt, and was clearly visible to everyone in the auditorium.

Principal Wentworth stared down at the flutists. They raised their flutes to their lips.

"Here comes your solo," the lady beside Riley said to him. "Don't mess this up."

Two things surprised Riley. First, that the woman could speak, and secondly, that he knew the song on the song sheet. My Heart Will Go On, the song from Charlotte's favourite movie Titanic. Since meeting Scoops, she had done nothing but belt it out in her room loud enough for the entire house to hear.

He raised his flute to his lips like a champ.

Principal Wentworth counted them in again. "1-2-3-4," he whispered as he waved his baton like a leaf blowing in a soft breeze. His left hand hung down by his side, fingers crossed.

He had no idea what was going to happen when they got to Riley's solo, but he couldn't panic. The show had to go on.

The flutists, save Riley, who was still pretending, played the soft intro beautifully. The strings joined in slowly during the second bar. Where Celine's melody started piano took over. The heads in the crowd started to sway from side to side like ripples of icy cold water on a tragic, solemn night.

Even Randle and Todd stood at the edge of the stage, mesmerized by the beautiful melody.

It was almost too nice for Scoops. Besides a few random "Why Does the Heart Go On?" vocal harmonies he was surprisingly behaving himself.

Scoops was just about to liven things up a bit by crashing the cymbal when he caught sight of Emily staring glossy-eyed at Riley. Riley was staring back at her as he majestically played the flute to her as if they were the only two people in the room.

Scoops moved his eyes over a seat and fixed his gaze on Lisa. She was looking right back at him! His heart skipped a beat. Could this be real?

Beside her, Dr. Fiore looked fast asleep, but every once in a while, he swirled his head around in a circle like he was floating along with the gentle sound waves.

Instantly, every instrument cut out except the flutes. Riley was too busy staring into Emily's eyes trying to communicate telepathically how much he loved her to notice.

Wentworth was just about to lead them into the bridge.

Riley had forgotten all about his solo until the lady beside him started wood pecking her knee against his thigh.

Scoops, driven by sheer passion, wrangled the gaunt timpanist's mallets from him and shoved him backstage. Almost as if he knew what he was doing, Scoops came in with a solid drum roll leading the rest of the orchestra back into the bridge.

The lady next to Riley continued to hit him frantically with her knee as if by some miracle Riley had learned how to blow into a flute, read sheet music, and become a musical virtuoso in the last ten minutes just in time for the ballad's crescendo.

Riley did the only thing that came to mind. Driven by Scoops rhythmic prowess that stirred the passion in his soul and ignited the desire in his heart for Emily, he bolted to his feet.

He dropped the flute to the floor and sang as loud as humanly possible...

"YOOOOOOU'RE HEEEEERE, THEEEEERE'S NOTHING I FEEEEEEAR,"

Wentworth froze in awe. Riley was right on key. His pitch was perfect.

Half of the orchestra stopped playing to listen to Riley.

Riley continued. "AND I KNOW THAT MY HEART WILL GO ON,"

Scoops pounded on the timpani as if he were a rock star in a band's farewell tour.

Riley took a deep breath so he could reach the high notes, "WEEEEE'LL STAAAAAAY FOREEEEEEVER THIS WAAAAAY YOU ARE SAFE IN MY HEART, AND MY HEART WILL GO ON AND ON!"

The crowd began to rise to its feet in a standing ovation.

As the band finished playing the outro Riley jumped off the stage running up the aisle towards Emily.

Emily brushed past Dr. and Mrs. Fiore and met him with a tight embrace.

Apart from Principal Wentworth's profuse sweating, the room was nearly silent.

The old woman in the front row began wiping tears from her eyes.

"Brilliant!" the old man in the front row yelled and jumped to his feet. "Absolutely brilliant!" he roared at the top of his lungs. "I have never seen or heard anything like it. BRAVO!"

The crowd erupted in applause.

While everyone gleefully watched Riley spin Emily around, Randle and Todd had Scoops in a tight embrace of their own backstage.

"Lisa!" he choked, but it was no use. He couldn't get the sound out. Lisa was too far away to save him.

"You're going to get another beating Scoops," Todd said. "I knew we should have finished you off when we had the chance."

The rest of the orchestra stayed in their places wondering what was going on.

The announcer came back on.

Could we please have the audience back to their seats? The show is not over.

The Not So Encore

Principal Wentworth was still standing on his platform, telling the audience that the performance wasn't done. "We still have more songs," he shouted at them. He waved his baton at the crowd trying to restore order as if they were a bunch of misbehaving high school students. They slowly stopped clapping and returned to their seats.

All except Ms. Fitzpatrick, who was desperately searching up and down the aisles for Mr. Wiggles.

"Ma'am," Cliff said, grasping her by the arm. "Please sit down."

"I have lost my kitten," she said, swatting his arm away. "My poor, Mr. Wiggles."

"Cat? How did you get a cat in here?" Cliff asked astonished.

"Mr. Wiggles," she repeated.

"Come with me," he ordered her, and he slowly guided her out of the auditorium.

Riley and Emily waved to the crowd and walked down the aisle to the exit as if they were leaving their wedding reception and heading on a two-week honeymoon. They burst through the doors and Riley pulled Emily into the still vacant coat check.

"What is going on?" Emily giggled as she wrapped her arms tightly around Riley's neck.

Riley laughed. "We came to your rescue!"

"Do you even know how to play the flute?"

"Yes," Riley's eyes narrowed. "Why, you didn't hear me playing?" He brushed a small tuft of hair out of her warm blue eyes then quickly put his arm around the small of her back.

"Well, no," she admitted cracking a wide smile, "I guess I couldn't hear anyone."

Riley laughed. "Tsk, tsk. All that hard work I put in to try and impress you."

"You were faking it, weren't you?"

Riley laughed. "Well, maybe just a little bit."

Emily threw her head back, closed her eyes, and smiled. Then she looked at him firmly. "What else are you faking, Mr. Kushinski?"

"That I am not absolutely crazy about you."

Emily looked deep into Riley's eyes then laughed. "Well, you're not good at faking that either. I knew that from the moment we first met."

Riley's heart was beating out of his chest. It was now or never. He leaned forward and gave her a soft kiss on the lips.

Emily leaned back and eyed him curiously. "Really, is that all you got?"

Riley laughed and softly put his hand on her cheek, pulling her in for a long, passionate smooch.

The auditorium was almost under control. Principal Wentworth fixed his wig and turned back to the orchestra. Finally, it was quiet. He raised his hands in the air.

"AHHHH CHOOO!" Miss Carpenter sneezed. This time, it was enough to knock her red wig clear off.

Mr. Wiggles (also known as Mrs. Fiore's cat) leaped from behind the stage, tore through the brasses, ran under the piano and jumped across Rhonda's lap into the trombones.

Rhonda dropped her tuba, jumped up on her swollen ankles, and screamed, "Rat!"

The bassoons and the clarinets jumped to their feet, echoing her cries. Some hopped up on their chairs while the brave started swinging their woodwinds like golf clubs trying to hit anything that moved.

Principal Wentworth looked out into the auditorium and to his horror watched as his audience dissipated through the exits.

"Who is that making that racket?" he screamed into the crowd.

Miss Carpenter let out another explosive sneeze.

"You!" he said, pointing at the culprit. His eyes widened as he saw it was Miss Carpenter. "You!"

Principal Wentworth turned and looked at the strange tall man beside her. Miss Carpenter's last sneeze had knocked Mr. Tillweed's mustache lose.

"And you!" he screamed at Mr. Tillweed when he recognized him. Mr. Wentworth began to crawl off the stage to chase after them.

The science teacher and the librarian jumped up as fast as they could and sprinted for the exits. They made it to the door just as Wentworth stumbled and fell in the middle of the aisle. He rolled back and forth, trying to build up enough momentum to get back on his feet. As he pushed himself to his knees, he whipped his sweat-soaked wig at them as they escaped into the lobby.

Alone backstage, Scoops continued fighting off his adversaries. Lisa was still in the auditorium enthralled by the chaos.

"Let him go," a tiny voice said behind them.

Scoops wrestled away to turn and see who had come to his rescue. It was Flynn.

"You guys are not fill-ins," Flynn said, pointing to Randle and Todd.

Scoops used Flynn's distraction to wiggle his way free. "Yeah, you guys are not musicians."

"Neither are you," the kid said sharply to Scoops.

Scoops started backing away from the three as if they had him cornered in a dark alley. "Well, I wouldn't say that exactly. I thought I was good. We'll have to wait and read the reviews."

The gaunt little timpanist joined in and made it a foursome.

Scoops picked up the pace and continued to back out onto the empty stage.

"Careful with this guy," Scoops said jokingly, "never play another man's timpani."

The man snarled as if he was a hungry stray. He lunged at Scoops and Scoops turned to run away colliding face first into the cymbals.

They crashed throughout the auditorium.

Mr. Wentworth had just barely made it back on his feet, and the loud noise startled him sending him spiraling back down the aisle like a cargo plane in a nosedive.

Lisa looked in the direction of the cymbals and saw Scoops. She instantly realized he was in trouble, jumped over her parents, and rushed out into the lobby.

Dr. Fiore stayed sitting as if by some miracle, the disaster was only a nightmare and the orchestra would continue playing as if nothing had happened.

Riley was just about to give Emily another big kiss when she saw Lisa running for the backstage door.

"What's going on?" Emily yelled after her.

"Scoops!" she cried, not breaking stride. "He needs me!" she yelled over her shoulder as she jump kicked the door open.

As Emily chased after Lisa, Riley decided to take the alternate route back through the auditorium doors. As he pulled them open, Principal Wentworth came crashing through falling to the lobby floor in a barrel roll.

"Great show, sir!" Riley yelled back at the sprawling principal and continued to run into the theatre.

"Kushinski!" Wentworth screamed out behind him.

As Riley bounded down the aisle, he almost tripped over Ms. Fitzpatrick. In the commotion, she had escaped from Cliff and made her way back into the theatre to continue her quest to find Mr. Wiggles. She sat crying on the floor, holding Principal Wentworth's wig.

"Riley," she said. "Look what they have done." She patted the wig and began to bawl. "The madding crowd has trampled my Mr. Wiggles."

Scoops had managed to get to his knees and was frantically crawling underneath the violinist's chairs to make it to the edge of the stage. "Riley!" he called out.

Behind him, Randle and Todd followed clearing a path through chairs and music stands as if they were sickling through a field of wheat.

Riley looked from Ms. Fitz to Scoops. Then from Scoops to Ms. Fitz. He faced a real Sophie's choice, or was it? Not really, he thought quickly.

"Ms. Fitz!" Riley shouted at her. "That is not Mr. Wiggles. That is Principal Wentworth's wig." He turned and ran towards Scoops, content that he had solved the dilemma.

Behind him, Ms. Fitz lifted the wig to her nose, smelled it and then swiftly tossed it aside as if the thought of a sweaty wig was much worse than that of a freshly trampled cat pelt.

As Riley reached the stage, Scoops jumped to him like a small child out of a burning window into the arms of a firefighter. Both of them crashed to the floor.

"Well, look who it is," Randle said, "Adele." He cracked his knuckles as if he were a pugilist getting ready to fight. "Quite a set of pipes you have on you, Riley."

Todd jumped in just in case there was any confusion, "yeah, and by pipes, we don't mean muscles."

"Thanks for clarifying," Riley said as he pushed Scoops' leg off him.

Behind them, Ms. Fitzpatrick continued to call for Mr. Wiggles. She walked out the door like a lost sheep out to pasture.

Lisa and Emily finally made it onto the stage behind Randle and Todd. Bill, Cliff, Rhonda, and an exasperated Principal Wentworth followed them. The rest of the auditorium had cleared out except Emilio and Lisa's mom, who had started to make their way up the aisle to the stage.

"There they are!" Rhonda croaked pointing at Riley and Scoops. They pushed past Randle and Todd and stopped at the edge of the stage to look down at the boys still sitting on the floor.

Scoops sat crossed legged as if he was waiting for a school assembly to start.

"Yeah that's them," Cliff said. "Those are the boys." He turned to Bill. "How did they get in?"

"They had tickets," Bill said in his raspy voice.

"Yeah, we had tickets," Riley repeated, trying his best to help.

"Two in fact," Scoops inserted nodding as if he was backing up Riley's statement.

"Not backstage tickets," Bill said, turning the tables on Cliff. "How did they get backstage? How did they get on stage?"

Cliff stood on his tiptoes and spoke as confidently and strong as he could muster. "They said they were getting cigarettes for Rhonda." He was at least three feet shorter than Bill, but that didn't intimidate him. "From you!"

"What are you implying?" he shot back at the little usher.

"Alright, alright," Principal Wentworth interjected. "Take it outside. Or better yet, start packing this place up!"

He turned and looked at Randle and Todd, then down at Riley and Scoops. "What is going on here?" he snarled. "You're all in big trouble."

"We didn't do anything," Randle and Todd pleaded their innocence.

"We didn't do anything either, sir." Scoops said. "We just wanted to spend some quality time with you."

"Yep," Riley added with a giant smile. "The best night of our lives, an evening with Principal Wentworth!"

Wentworth started to overheat. The boys could almost see the steam rising off his shiny head. "Who are you?" he shot at Lisa's parents.

Riley made the introduction, "this is Dr. Fiore."

"Emilio," Scoops inserted helpfully.

"My dad," Lisa added.

Dr. Fiore stepped forward. "Good show, conductor." He outstretched his hand. "It was exceptional."

"Really?" Principal Wentworth asked, surprised.

"Yeah, really?" Lisa repeated.

"What a finale, I have never seen anything like it. I found your approach quite refreshing."

Wentworth's tone changed. "Well, thank you, sir."

Dr. Fiore continued. It was clear that his knowledge of classical music did not equate to his knowledge of cars and racing. "These boys did quite a great job, must have practiced the whole act a lot. I thought they were just a bunch of troublemakers."

"Nope," Scoops said, shaking his head from side to side.

"Not us, sir," Riley added.

Dr. Fiore looked sternly at Scoops. "And to think you would have skipped all this to spend time with my Lisa. I may have underestimated you."

Lisa's mom stared in disbelief at her clueless husband. She looked at Lisa and Emily, who were grinning from ear to ear.

"Keep it up, boys. You have a future in this business. You too conductor," he gave Principal Wentworth a wink as if he were a talent scout.

Randle and Todd tried to interject, but Scoops beat them to the punch.

"Hey look!," Scoops said.

Cowering under a row of seats next to him was Mrs. Fiore's tabby cat.

"I think this belongs to you ma'am," Scoops said as he softly picked up the cat and took it to her.

She screamed in delight. "It does, it does!" she ran and grabbed it from Scoops. She was so happy she gave Scoops a big kiss on the cheek. "We must get her home now, Emilio."

"Her?" Scoops looked at Riley as they walked away.

"Who knew?" Riley said. "Somebody should tell Ms. Fitz Mr. Wiggles is actually Ms. Wiggles."

They both laughed.

"Come with me," Principal Wentworth said to Todd. "We could use a big strapping boy like you to help load equipment." He then turned and looked awkwardly at Randle, "and I guess I can find something for you to do."

"But sir," Randle whined, looking for Emily and Lisa who had already jumped off the stage. "What about Riley and Scoops?"

"I will deal with them on Monday," he said winking at Riley as if to say thanks.

"But sir, Riley and Scoops—"

"Now!" Principal Wentworth snarled at Randle.

Todd and Randle jumped and immediately started following the big man backstage.

Behind them, Flynn was already starting to bark orders.

Scoops smiled at Riley, "I think Principal Wentworth has a crush on you. I saw that wink. I bet he is a big Celine fan."

Riley just shook his head.

"You know, you should really thank me," Scoops continued. "I'm the one that made sure you came in on key with those kettle drums."

Riley laughed and put his arm around Emily. "Yeah, you can really play those."

Lisa cozied up to Scoops, "you can play my kettle drums anytime."

"Your what?" Dr. Fiore yelled at them.

"Her kettle drums sir, her kettle drums," Scoops proudly announced and held his hand up to high five Riley.

Riley, Emily, and Lisa's faces froze, anticipating Dr. Fiore's eruption.

Manufactured by Amazon.ca
Bolton, ON